Return to Darlo

By

Maurice Horner

About The Author

Maurice Horner was born in Darlington and ended up as one of its exports as soon as he left school. He now lives in New Zealand.

He was pleased to have been raised in one of Durham's finest towns at a time when the old order was changing. At a national, indeed an international level, the Beatles were testing servitude and blazing new trails with 'can do' attitudes. Within the town Harry Evans was taking the Northern Echo to new heights and making people not only stop and think but do something about the wrongs and injustices of the world. And those lucky enough to be tutored and guided by J. L. (Dickie) Bird found themselves no longer able to take anything for granted ever again.

The comedy, zest, pathos, first encountered in Tales of Darlo is back in Return to Darlo. And life continues.

First Printing, 2020

ISBN-9780473547219 (EPUB)
ISBN-9780473545673 (PRINTED)

The first book in the Series

Tales of Darlo
is available at
www.bookdepository.com/Tales-of-Darlo/9781977930989

Anyone wishing to contact the author may do so at
rtntodarlo@outlook.co.nz

Contents

Introduction

The old woman asked for "six measures of brandy, please," as she hands over a freshly rinsed bottle that's been kept at the back of the cupboard for such occasions. A shot for each of the pallbearers to warm them up and ward off the morbidity of the graveyard.

"Have you any silver threepenny bits in your change Mister Arkwright?" asks another old woman at the grocers as she searches for an increasingly rare commodity to put in the hands of a new born to protect it from the evils of this world, and the next as well, if it's sickly.

The town hall clock, strikes the hour as it stands erect like a broody hen watching over its offspring, watching them come and seeing them go.

Beneath its passive stare it has seen its wards meet, fight, love, cry, celebrate, and on the steps beside it leading up to the market, argue their political ideals. And the wards remember that it was under the town clock they met their friends before going to the pub, the dance, the party or where they'd met their husband or wife. And it was under the town hall clock they first heard that John F. Kennedy was assassinated.

The town hall clock presided over the angry crowds as they futilely protested about losing their engineering works and livelihoods. It watched as the new mayoral car swished by, bearing the badge of the company setting up its new subsidised factory on the edge of town.

It saw the once thriving shops that sold merchandise of every type and desire slowly devolve into purveyors of second-hand goods for the benefit of one charity or another.

It watched as part of its brood left for university, for jobs and opportunities the town could no longer offer. It watched over the drugs being dealt in St Cuthbert's churchyard. It noticed the lookouts posted in the lane that contained the historic but nondescript Elizabethan wall running between Tubwell Row and the marketplace.

It watched as those who went away, came back for family, for friends, to lick wounds, and sometimes to stay.

And beside the road built to avoid the town there sits a brick locomotive locked in a permanent siding, gushing out steam and smoke that will take it nowhere.

Chapter One
The Funeral

It was a sombre day with grey skies brooding a chilly dampness. Foolhardy ones who were out without an overcoat had ruddy faces mottled with yellowy white patches, their lips narrow and pinched shut. They hugged and rubbed themselves or stomped to keep warm.

Sean, or Crud as he was known to those he'd grown up with, headed across the graveyard towards the chapel. He wasn't quite sure what he was doing there. He'd come back to his hometown to lick his wounds before moving on again.

He didn't normally read the births, marriages, and deaths

column in the newspaper or as his mother called them, the hatch, match, and despatches. Maybe it was just his mood but for whatever reason he'd ended up looking at the list of those who had recently died. As he read down, he noticed that Matty had died.

He didn't at first cotton on that it was someone he knew but his curiosity was aroused when he noticed the date of birth and a mention of his old school in the obituary. He initially thought it unfair that amongst the mass of those who'd had a fair innings that there was someone of his own age who had proved to be mortal. There was no mention of illness or accident in the death notice, it just didn't seem right. It was only then, as he looked further at the notice, that he realised he knew him. That's right, they'd been at school together. Although not close, he was an affable lad and since school Sean had run into him from time to time and wasted away a couple of hours catching up on contemporaries and generally putting the world to rights.

Sean walked through the doorway of the chapel into the muffled, shuffling and whispering atmosphere common to funerals. A sotto voce organ dirged away in the background. He sat on one of the pews at the side and somewhat towards the rear, anonymity was fine with him, after all he wasn't that close. Besides which he didn't want to talk, he didn't want to explain to anyone what he was doing back in the town. And he equally didn't want to explain to those who hadn't even realised he'd left town in the first place.

It didn't seem too bad a turn out for poor Matty thought Sean. As people drifted in, the chapel seemed a good half-full. The coffin looked lonely propped up on its trestles at the front with a wreath on top. After that Sean kept his eyes cast downwards, he wasn't being deliberately reverential, he just wanted to isolate himself from the grief of others. Even more so when someone came to sit alongside on the pew. He bowed his head a little further to ignore them.

"Hi up, Sean," came a loud whispered voice to his right. He looked up and turned his head.

"Good grief, Ducka, what are you doing here?"

As Ducka was about to speak the organ grew in crescendo to signal the start of the service. The conversation had to wait.

Both Sean and Ducka stood up and sat down, along with everyone else, as dictated by the tempo of the funeral service. They listened to the eulogies and felt somewhat uncomfortable when the deliverers were overcome with emotion and broke into sobs. Words spoken that would have been better told to Matty when he was alive, thought Sean. At last the service came to its conclusion and everyone was invited to the Red Lion.

They stood solemnly but with a sense of impatience as the coffin was led back through the chapel on its way to the hearse and crematorium.

Ducka and Sean slowly shuffled towards the exit showing deference to one and all who wished to be in front of them. As they emerged into the daylight, they edged away from the those crowding around Matty's parents offering their condolences. At last they stood to one side with a bit of space around them.

"Ducka, is it me or is someone taking the piss?" asked Sean quietly.

"What do you mean?"

"Well look at the size of the coffin," said Sean, "and look at the size of his parents. His dad would need high heels and a pair of ladders to reach five feet and his mother could have been a Munchkin in the Wizard of Oz. As I remember Matty was no taller than them. We didn't call him Tiny for nothing. So why a coffin that would house Goliath?"

"I understand that's what killed him," said Ducka.

"What? Goliath? Come off it or are you telling me Goliath jumped on him from a great height and flattened him such that he was bigger than Ben Hur thus necessitating the need for a big coffin. If that were the case then you'd expect the coffin to be six-foot-long, five feet wide and two inches high.

"No, you silly sod. You know he had a thing about his height and wanted to be taller. Well, I'm told, he went to the doctor because he'd heard you could have an operation that could make your legs longer. Anyway, the doctor said that all that would do would be to make him look like a circus midget on stilts. Matty's disappointment was quickly overcome by the doctor telling him there was a new treatment and prescribed growth hormones. They worked and he grew but it turned out that not everything was what it was cracked up to be. There was a problem with the way the hormone had been manufactured from cattle. Sadly, it was the treatment that killed him and hence the big coffin."

"Sounds like a tall story to me," said Sean mischievously. "Red Lion?"

"Aye, why not?"

As the hearse and immediate family headed towards the crematorium the conversations of those left behind transited from its reverential tones and elevated into normal chatter. Laughter started to be heard and soon became a general part of the hubbub.

Sean and Ducka reflected on the town as they walked towards the Red Lion. It was nice to be back and see some old familiar places, but not to stay. They thought nothing had changed much and, in some respects, it seemed to be getting worse. A young woman had been raped in daylight walking near the Methodists' Chapel, not too far from the centre of town. The girl's parents had been criticised for not being with her. Both agreed something was wrong when a young woman could not safely walk along a comparatively main road without being attacked. Surely people should have been discussing how to make the town safer and not alleging parental inadequacies. It was an abrogation; an excuse was being created to avoid civic responsibility. Both heartedly agreed on the subject.

Sean and Ducka walked into the pub, picked up a pint and were encouraged to tuck into the sandwiches and sausage rolls. They exchanged the odd pleasantry with other attendees which usually amounted to a reflection on the day's weather. They agreed with everyone notwithstanding that people had different opinions about it.

"It's been a lovely day for the funeral. Good that the rains kept off."

"Yes, yes it has."

"The weather could have been better for him. It's been a bit cold and miserable."

"Yes, yes, it has."

"It's drear isn't it? Just what you need for a funeral. Shows that those above us care."

"Aye, that's right."

After Matty's parents joined the wake from the crematorium Sean and Ducka paid their respects then retreated to a table in the corner with their pints and a plate of sausage rolls.

"So, what you doing back here, Sean? I thought you'd moved off."

"Well, I had, I mean I have. I've just come back for a couple of weeks to lick my wounds."

"Why? What's gone on?"

"My marriage broke down."

"I'm sorry to hear it, Sean."

"Don't be, it's as well over and done with. You may

remember that before I moved down South for a job, I'd fallen
for a gorgeous woman called Pru. I mean I really and truly fell
for her. Unfortunately, she was married. I thought she was going
to leave her husband and come away with me. But that's what
thought did, thinking you're following a wedding procession
only to find out it's a funeral."

"Silly cow!" said Ducka.

"No, you can't say that about her, if you ever met her,
you'd know what I mean. Anyway, I moved down South and
met this bird in a pub after work one Friday. She looked a bit
like Pru, which is what attracted me to her. My new mates
down there had got into her ear and persuaded her I was some
sort of closet millionaire about to inherit a fortune. And before
you knew it, we were married. It didn't take long for me to
work out she wasn't Pru and for her to realise there was no
hidden fortune for her to spend on yet more clothes and shoes.
You would hardly know we had a bedroom floor; it was hidden
beneath the mound of her things littered all over the place."

"Doesn't sound the best."

"No, it wasn't. The final straw came when I found out that
as soon as I left through the front door to go to work, she was
letting in a string of lovers through the back door, including
the dustbin man. So, as you may guess the separation is a relief
all round."

"You've come back to look for Pru?"

"No, she made her decision and I'll respect it. I love her
too much to want to make her life a misery and that's all I'd
do if I turned up on her doorstep. I do still think about her a
lot. Anyway, less about me and how about you? What have you
been up to? Are you married? What are you doing back here?
And did you ever claim your free pint for hitchhiking further
than anyone else that weekend years ago?"

"Whoa, hold on, one question per breath please."

"Sorry, please answer all the above questions, together with those that should be asked, in whatever order you like, using not more than six sentences, ten capital letters, five full stops, no question marks but as many exclamation marks or commas as you like. Starting from now," Sean said in a mock television quizmaster's tone.

"Last things first, I did call in to the old King's Head, but Sam has moved on. He's bought a hostelry somewhere up the dales and has established a well-regarded restaurant and has accommodation as well, I was told. I asked his replacement for a pint of his warmest, but the beer was quickly chilled with the reception I got, there was a definite sense of humour failure." Ducka sat back and supped his beer.

"What else was it you wanted to know? What am I doing back here was one of your questions?" he paused for a moment. "The old man's not too well, he suffers from emphysema, partly caused by all that crap he used to breathe in where he worked but more so by his smoking those dreadful Woodbines, the killer of all ciggies. And will he give it up? No! The silly sod says it's the only pleasure he gets in life. What pleasure you can get from hacking and coughing your lungs out every morning, I don't know." Ducka sounded very frustrated by it all.

"Aye, there's not much you can do to help folk when they won't help themselves," said Sean sympathetically.

"When I tell him off and tell him what he should do for his own good all I get is this puppy dog look followed by, 'You'll miss me when I gone.' I tell him I'll get the tape measure out and start measuring him up, all of which results in one of his 'you're ungrateful' rants. Well, it takes his mind off other things and we end up having a good laugh at each other, at least until it starts him coughing again."

"You staying around long?"

"Nah, just a few days to see what I can do for the old folk then I'll be back to Munich."

"You been there long?"

"You mentioned that weekend when we all went hitchhiking to see who could travel the furthest. Once I'd started I just kept going. I suppose I was running away from Guy and Judy's deaths. I just wished I hadn't said what I did. I didn't really want their car to have a puncture and crash, killing them both. I didn't mean it. It's a bit like Waylon Jennings, just after he'd given up his seat on the aircraft to the Big Bopper, saying to Buddy Holly, 'I hope your plane crashes.' Even though it was meant as a funny quip at the time, you can't unsay those words and they live to haunt you. Anyway, I ended up in Bavaria and now have an engineering job on the outskirts of Munich."

"Married?"

"No, I have a girlfriend, but I don't think that's going to last much longer. She's into a bit of S and M and I'm not. It started when we were having it away one night. It was going great guns and we were heading towards the moment when the bells start to chime in Tchaikovsky's 1812. Suddenly she digs her nails into my back, and I mean digs her nails in. Goodness, it put me off my stroke. Anyway, bit by bit she's been winding this sort of thing up and it just doesn't do anything for me, in fact quite the reverse."

"So, no one serious?"

"Funnily enough, strange as it may seem, I met a girl from Richmond in Munich, she was working for a law firm. I really liked Stella, but I think she was running from greater demons than mine. She tackled life as if the world was going to end tomorrow and wanted to cram everything in before it happened. She had so much energy and enthusiasm, I couldn't keep up with her. She wore me out! But she was utterly wonderful."

"Do you still see her?"

"No. One day she was there and then, like a genie in a bottle, she disappeared, gone to find her next adventure, no doubt. I tried to track her down but the firm where she worked were not helpful."

The wake was starting to wind down. The lads tried to muffle their mirth as they overheard one of the attendees, suitably dressed in black, saying to Matty's mother on the way out, "Eee, sorry about your lad, but I have enjoyed me self."

"Well," said Sean, "with a sentiment like that I think it's time for us to move off. Let's go for a Chinese."

Chapter Two

Kipper's Bargain

Sean and Ducka settled down to await their Egg Foo Yung and Chop Suey. The meal included soup and they both looked at the cornflower glug put down before them and counted the pieces of carrot that looked lost in the white paste. Ducka asked if Sean had seen anyone else since he'd been back.

"I ran into Kipper yesterday. Do you remember him? Kipper Shipley."

"Aye, I remember hearing of him, used to work at the same engineers as you."

"That's him, he was a foreman there. If there was ever

a bit of a problem he'd come rushing in yelling, 'Don't panic, don't panic,' and he'd be the only one panicking. That's how he got his name, he was always flapping about. Ron was his given name. He was telling me that he and his wife, Lilly, had just come back from Paris."

"They were a funny couple," began Sean. "They have been married for over thirty years. I'd heard they had drifted into it in the dim and distant past. Most of their friends were already married so there was a feeling they should as well. Even the proposal was a bit of a haze. Ron had used some of his hectoring prowess that Lilly would get used to over the years which was particularly noticeable when she drove him around town. His incessant advice, both for reasons of safety and necessity, was totally ignored. Ron's sense of proposal had been to use the endearing argument of 'You'd better marry me 'cos no one else will want you.' Lilly, not known to have a large sense of self-worth, concurred.

They were an anonymous couple and were not renowned for standing out in a crowd, indeed, it is said, they hardly stood out at their own wedding. It was one of those self-catering affairs. They wondered about turning it into a 'bring-a-plate do' but the bride's mother objected and agreed to help by baking for the day including the chocolate wedding cake. She was good at chocolate cakes, she normally baked them for birthdays. Years later they had heard about the politician who married one fine morning. Following the wedding ceremony, guests were invited to attend a wedding breakfast at a nearby restaurant. The delightful thing was that as the guests departed, they were handed a bill for their food and drink. Ron and Lilly ruminated and only wished they'd had the courage to do the same.

It wasn't the sort of marriage where the word love featured a lot. There was sufficient affection, however, for them to produce a pigeon pair over time, a boy, and a girl. They were a shy pair of kids, but Ron and Lilly invested sufficiently in them hoping that they would look after them in their dotage. 'You will look after us when we get old, won't you?' was a question frequently dropped into their conversations with their children. They felt a sense of responsibility didn't hurt anyone. Whether it was this indoctrination or their innate shyness but whichever, the children didn't play a lot in the streets with the kids in their neighbourhood.

Over the years Ron and Lilly grew attached to each other. They felt as comfortable and as familiar together as a well-loved pair of old slippers. They had some things in common. They liked the same sort of television programmes and happily chirped away to each other across the strains of the channel they were watching. They particularly liked anything that used the word 'pussy' with a double-entendre. That was hilarious. They didn't mind repetitive humour and could happily watch the same programme again and again and were still able to laugh at the same bits. Their ways parted when it came to sport. Ron loved his sport. That was when Lilly took to her egg painting or a good Mills and Boon book.

They also enjoyed their food, good old fashioned comfort food, none of that nouveau-cuisine rubbish. Occasionally, if they felt a bit adventurous, they'd have a good feed at a Thai restaurant, but it had to be cheap enough and filling and preferably with a helping of chips. Their food helped them settle into a Pickwickian rotundness in life.

Sometimes they went for a Smorgasbord but made sure they had everything they could for what they had to pay. Such visits called for a bit of preparation beforehand. Lilly made sure she took her largest handbag and lined one of the compartments with a plastic bag. As she went around filling up her plate she kept her handbag open and slipped in a good few slices of ham. Ron did his bit. He'd fill his plate to overflowing and then when back at the table he would surreptitiously add more ham to the handbag under the table. When he was working this filled the sandwiches in his bait tin more than once. Now that he wasn't working the ham went straight into the freezer and when not used for snacks could quickly be turned into sandwiches for unexpected guests.

As may be gathered Ron and Lilly were careful with their money. It was the one area where they became passionate and really had something in common. They would search Heaven and Hell for a good bargain. A bargain was the one thing that had the blood rushing to their heads. In the good old days, when supermarkets closed at night, in the half hour before closing, all the bread, pastries and other goods that were coming to the end of their shelf life were marked down. They would rush in and fill up their trolley. It wasn't the same these days with supermarkets staying open for 24 hours; things could be marked down at any time of the day or night. There was now much more of an art in picking your day and shift to get the best results.

Not many people knew you could get trays of seconds from the egg factory and they were cheap. The fact that you sometimes had to open the eggs with scissors because they were more like turtle's eggs than hen's eggs was of no great consequence.

When Ron and Lilly finally plucked up sufficient courage to buy a new car, they would only ever buy a demonstrator or a run out model because they could save heaps that way. They did, however, regret the Lada. There were only so many jokes you could tell about a Lada, admittedly a lot, but only so many. For once repetitive humour did not have its appeal. Complete

strangers would confront them as they got out of their Lada
to share their latest Lada joke. It wasn't a laughing matter. As
people approached their car Ron started to have the first word,
'We've heard that one,' he'd say. 'But you don't know what I
was going to say.' 'We've heard them all,' would reply Ron. He
did feel a bit foolish when a chap had said, 'So you know your
lights at the back are not working. You should do something
about them.' The Lada did teach them that not all bargains were
what they were cracked up to be. The dealer they bought the
car from wouldn't let them have a test drive before buying it.
He asked them how they would feel about buying a car that
somebody else had driven. 'I mean to say, that's not a new car
is it?' intoned the salesman. At the time, they thought this was
a very good point and were pleased the dealer would think so
much of them to ensure they had a pristine car. After that they
insisted on having a test drive for any car they bought.

When they retired, they enjoyed going on holiday
particularly when it was the school term although they did query
the number of field trips pupils these days seemed to get away
with. Kids should be at school learning and not having another
holiday gallivanting about under the frantic misguidance of a
teacher or two. Why should they have their enjoyment impaired
by being subjected to these mini flash mobs?

Ron told me that when the weather was beginning to
take a turn for the worse, he and Lilly had decided to look
at going somewhere before it got too bad. Lilly's search for
bargain flights resulted in a cheap flight using Air Easy. There
was nothing wrong with Air Easy, their aircraft weren't the most
modern, but they hadn't had a crash for a long time. And if
you got those seats next to the toilets at the back then you had
a little more legroom. The staff were quite civil even if they
didn't understand a word you said. If you wanted food, you had

to buy it, but they didn't mind as they'd take their own ham sandwiches.

So, it was that six weeks later Ron and Lilly fetched up at a thin walled hotel in Paris. They could have rented the room by the hour if they had known it. They tended not to fly too well, particularly Lilly, and so they ended up being grumpy with each other. After the flight, all Lilly wanted to do was go straight to bed. She found herself walking up four floors to their room. The hotel did not have a lift.

Ron, on the other hand, went out for a walk. Night was for going to bed in his mind, albeit since retirement this didn't always work, but today he was going to try. With a map in hand from the hotel he set out to explore the streets in the neighbourhood. They had chosen to stay in the Marais, a district that seemed to have the reputation of being a bit rough, but it seemed alright to him. Just in case, he'd taken precautions, he only carried a minimal amount of money and kept his credit card in a separate pocket, wrapped in aluminium foil, 'It's to FOIL any scammers' he would chortle as an explanation to shopkeepers as he set about the task of unwrapping his card. He'd had Lilly lengthen the pockets on his trousers so that any pickpocket would have to reach to Australia before they found anything. They were so long he could scratch his knees with his hands still in his pockets.

The day was warm, and he was starting to feel a little tired after walking about for two or three hours. A couple of near misses by looking the wrong way before walking out on to the street, or 'rue' as he now liked to call them, had jolted him into being reasonably awake. He decided to call at a café and have a couple of beers before heading back to see if Lilly had woken up. From the café, it was a short saunter back to the hotel.

As he walked along, his way was suddenly blocked by a

young woman waving her arms and blowing him kisses. He was taken aback and stopped in his tracks.

'You want a good time with nice young lady?' enquired the young woman in a very French accented way.

Ron wondered how on earth she knew to address him in English. It couldn't be his shorts and white legs because he was wearing his long trousers.

'Very cheap for big boy like you,' persisted the young woman.

Ron dived into his pocket and produced a 10 franc note.

'I only have 10 francs. What do I get for 10 francs?'

'For 10 francs, you don't even get a peck. You lucky I even talk to you for 10 francs,' said the young woman. 'You no more money than that?' As she said that her hand felt his crotch.

This startled Ron who started to scurry away saying, 'No, no, no,' and hanging tightly onto his 10 francs.

He heard the young woman calling after him, 'You no get much for 10 francs around here Buster.'

Ron hurried back to the hotel. Lilly was just waking up as he entered the room. 'You been far?' she enquired.

'Just here and there,' replied Ron. He wasn't sure he'd tell her about the young woman feeling his crotch. She might think he'd egged her on. He'd wait until she was in a better frame of mind in a day or two.

After smartening up they decided to find a café for an evening meal. They walked out of the hotel and down the street looking for something that took their fancy. They were being very choosey. Dealing with a French menu could have its challenges; dealing with a Vietnamese menu in French was beyond them. As they turned a corner who should they run into but the young woman who had confronted Ron earlier.

The young woman stepped in front of Ron. She looked at

him. Then she looked very critically at Lilly.

'I told you, you no get much for 10 francs,' she said to Ron.

'Yes,' Ron replied, 'she is a bargain, my bargain.' And escorted a flummoxed Lilly down the road to an English pub selling fish and chips with the nearest thing the French could manage to mushy peas.

And that" said Sean, "is the story of Lilly and Ron." The soup plates with their half-eaten contents were being cleared away.

"If the next course is as bad as that soup, we might have cause to go and visit Kipper and ask for one of his ham sandwiches," said Ducka with a smile on his face.

Chapter Three
Going to the Dogs

As the Foo Yung and Chop Suey arrived on the table Sean was asking Ducka if he'd met with anyone else from the old days.

"Yes, I ran into Maureen a couple of days ago."

"How's she doing?"

"Alright by the sounds. She married Chris Or and they have a small holding just down the road towards Neasham."

"You don't mean Chris Either Or, the chap that had difficulty making his mind up."

"That's him."

"How did they meet?"

Ducka told Sean that he understood that they had first met through a cyclists' touring club. The group Maureen was riding with had become spread out along the dale's road. She had been enjoying the countryside and was towards the rear when she came across Chris at a crossroads trying to decide which road he should take. Maureen took him under her wing and rode with him back to town. From then on they became increasingly happy with each other's company.

Maureen had put Chris out of his misery when he proposed in his circumspect way. He had pondered how nice it would be if they were to get married but, on the other hand, if they didn't, he wouldn't mind, providing they remained friends. And if they did decide to get married it could be soon or in a couple of years' time or whenever, whatever would suit Maureen. Maureen had cut the monologue short by telling Chris she would.

Chris loved dogs and had a wonderful way with them and carried an authority when working with canines that seemed lacking in his own world. And so, they decided to buy a small holding just out of town and establish kennels.

It was hard work, but they were making a go of it. Maureen kept her job with the council and helped in the kennels both before and after work. They made a reasonable living between the pair of them and were slowly paying off the mortgage. They would have liked children but didn't think they could afford them. They needed to do something more to earn some extra money.

As they had a big vegetable garden Maureen thought about selling their surplus at the roadside. She also set about pickling some of the produce to sell at the town market.

Chris built a roadside stall with an honesty box as they

couldn't be in attendance all the time. They found out that not
all people are honest and were dejected when someone stole
not just the money but the honesty box as well. The final nail
was put in the coffin when they were warned about the dangers
of people stopping in the road to buy from the stall.

The pickling venture didn't fare much better. After
allowing for the cost of jars and hiring the market stall they
weren't much better off. It was back to the drawing board.

As they ran kennels and dogs were coming and going at
regular intervals Maureen got out her sewing machine and
started to make coats for dogs. With a steady supply of potential
customers through the door she felt sure she was onto a winner.
She soon learnt that people dropping their dogs off didn't want
to hang around before going on their holidays and when they
came back to collect their pooch they were so busy making a
fuss of them that any other distractions were to be ignored. It
was back to the drawing board again.

It was one of Chris's customers called Derek, who gave
them their next idea. He left a couple of greyhounds for them
to look after when he went on holiday. They were taken with
the dogs and got chatting to Derek when he returned to pick
them up. He raced them and said you could make a penny
or two if you picked a good dog and trained it well. So, with
Derek's help they bought a pup, called it Bunny Runner, and
started to train it. Maureen fed the dog and petted it, Chris took
it for long walks and encouraged it to run.

When Bunny Runner was a bit older, they started to train
it more seriously by going into the field at the back of their
small holding to race him there. Chris would take him to one
end of the field whilst Maureen went to the other. She carried
a packet of dog biscuits. When all was ready Chris would release
Bunny Runner from his lead and raise his arm. This was a signal

to Maureen to start calling him.

"Buuuuunnnnny, Bunny, Bunny, Bunny," she sang in a descending crescendo. This, she kept repeating until the dog reached her. It was rewarded with dog biscuits, hugs and pats all reinforced with, "Who's a good boy then? Who's a good boy?"

As the dog matured and its speed improved, they brought in Derek to see what he thought. They measured the distance across the field's diagonal and put a stopwatch on Bunny's run. They did it three times with Derek noting down the times. Derek did some quick calculations and gave them advice on what they could do to help Bunny improve his performance.

After three such visits Derek deemed that the dog was ready for its first serious race, he thought Bunny had a nice turn of speed. He recommended to them that they enter their dog in a novice race that was coming up at the local track. He said that the dogs had to become accustomed to the atmosphere of a track and that it was better to start off modestly and then build them up for bigger races.

So, it was that one Saturday night, three weeks later, Chris was tucking Bunny into a trap while Maureen stood proudly ringside about half-way along the back straight. She wanted to see how Bunny would both start and finish as well as run along the straight. Both her and Chris had great expectations for Bunny and their fortunes. All seemed to augur well.

Bunny came out of the trap with gusto and was soon leading the pack by three quarters of a length. It was all very exciting. Maureen was surprised how she was taken with the whole atmosphere and all the shouting and cheering she was hearing. She soon found herself joining in.

"Buuuuunnnnny, Bunny, Bunny, Bunny," she yelled in gay abandonment, again and again. She couldn't contain herself until as the dogs neared where she stood Bunny suddenly deviated and ran off the track straight to where she was.

Which is why Chris banned Maureen from the track. But without the encouragement of Maureen's titbits Bunny never reached the potential expected of him.

This also explains why Chris and Maureen have a pet greyhound.

Not long afterwards a rest home developer bought their small holding and so they bought another one further away but with some savings in the bank their thoughts have turned to starting a family.

"Aye, I've sometimes wondered what it would be like having a kid," said Sean, "a little curly haired red head running around my feet and over the fields, but I reckon I'd make a crap dad."

"You never know," said Ducka. "You never know."

Chapter Four
The Misunderstanding

As they waited for their fruit salad with evaporated milk to appear Ducka changed the subject.

"I remember, Sean, that when you left school you were eager to get away from this town and went to sea. I was always surprised when you came back. You didn't seem to have been away too long. Didn't the sea suit?"

"It was a combination of things. Going to sea didn't live up to my romantic notions. It was far more boring than I ever imagined. I shipped as an engineering cadet, in other words a general dogsbody. And when you got to a port you would find yourself docked miles from anywhere. I shipped out on a line that ran from Liverpool to the eastern seaboard of the States. The ship was a tramp so once we arrived in the States we'd find ourselves going up and down the coast looking for sufficient cargo to come home again. I didn't really see much of the country."

"So, what about every sailor's dream of having a girl in every port?" asked Ducka.

"That was the other reason for me coming home and being discharged. I met a girl who came to one of our onboard parties. She was a great relief from living alongside a bunch of stinky sailors. We got on great, exchanged addresses and vowed to keep in touch when the ship moved on. But it wasn't to be. I found out shortly afterwards that I had a dose of the pox. The Line got me some medical treatment in the US and then flew me home and gave me my discharge papers with a 'don't call us we'll call you message'. So, I was back home and not allowed a drink for a couple of months while I had the treatment. Leastwise, I obtained some grounding in engineering that helped me land a job once I was back."

"I didn't know that" said Ducka, "I'd heard that it was just the monotony of being at sea that got to you."

"Well I wasn't going to brag about having VD, was I? What love life I aspired to would have been quickly knocked on the head."

"A bit like Dot in a way," said Ducka.

"Why? What happened there?"

"Poor Dot, I don't know if you remember but she had fallen for an engineer who ended up getting a job with one of the petroleum companies in the Middle East. Before he took off, they announced their engagement. It was all sweetness, light and roses. After he'd been out there for a few months he came home on leave and the romance not only carried on from where they'd left off but flourished. The only problem was after he returned to the Middle East. Dot found that he'd left her with a lovely present, a dose of the clap. It was a tough way to find out that he wasn't being exactly faithful to her. Not surprisingly she ended the engagement, but it took her a while to get over it."

"What the clap?"

"No, you silly sod," said Ducka, "the broken heart."

"Break ups are never pleasant but I suppose the quicker and cleaner it is, the better. Seeing a couple grinding away the last vestiges of love is painful," added Sean. "It's like watching a slow-motion train wreck. You can see what is going to happen and there's nothing you can do about it. There was a couple I came across down south, Gerry and Mandy, whose marriage, foundered on the rocks, against all predictions. When I first came across them, they were a very together couple who would fiercely stick up for each other which is why, given a peculiar logic, they were known as the Gerrymanderers.

They had been married for close on fifty years and seemingly had had a happy marriage. It was close to their anniversary and they had decided to catch up with their best man, groomsman and Ruth, Mandy's chief bridesmaid. Ruth and Mandy had been best friends for many years but like a lot of relationships with old friends, they had grown apart over the years as each had gone down their own paths and chased their own dreams. Notwithstanding, it was good catching up with everyone and they relived their former days and caught up with all their derring-dos since. In some ways, it was obvious that life hadn't been as kind to Ruth as she would have wished. The small fortune she had inherited had disappeared and she was the only one of them still needing to work to make ends meet.

As they sat there, Ruth turned to Gerry and asked if he

knew everything his wife had got up to all those years ago. Gerry batted the enquiry away by saying that if he needed to know he was sure Mandy would have told him. And so, the conversation moved on.

Later, after they had said their farewells and were on their own Gerry said to his wife that he thought it was rather naughty if not mischievous of Ruth to have asked the question. Mandy had replied that everyone has their secrets and they should be left in the past.

That was the start of it, after this they noticeably became more distant with each other. When you caught up with them separately, they would each start to open-up about this and that. Neither of them wanted to listen, just to talk.

Mandy recalled the day of their anniversary when she had caught up with her friend Ruth. She thought she hadn't worn well and was surprised she had stayed with her husband. In Mandy's mind he was a wastrel. But Ruth seemed to accept her lot. She'd drive him to the pub every Sunday lunchtime and pick him up later, in the meantime she would have cleaned the house. She was still working fulltime whilst he had retired. Mandy thought it should have been him looking after the house for her. Ruth seemed resigned to her life, but Mandy wondered if she detected a hint of jealousy, even resentment. Maybe, but hopefully she was just imagining it.

Gerry also recalled their anniversary, but it is what was said at the end that bothered him. 'We all have our secrets and they should be left in the past.' For some reason, he couldn't get it out of his mind. He'd tell you that he'd never knowingly kept any secrets from Mandy; their marriage was based on openness and trust. Surely, she hadn't kept secrets from him. And if so, he wondered if it really mattered. They had been together for half a century and it had been a relationship of happiness and togetherness like few others they knew. Even this year they had been on a coach tour and some of the people thought they were newly married. It was a loving relationship.

Mandy said that she recognised the signs. He was becoming quiet. She knew they were going to have one of those periods when he became morose and would hardly say a word. She decided to keep out of his way until he became his old self again. Thankfully, it didn't happen too often but when it did, what a pain!

Gerry fretted. He'd argue with you that if she had secrets, didn't that betray the whole of their relationship, had it been built on a false foundation? She shouldn't have kept secrets. You'd ask him if she had secrets from so long ago, should they matter? You'd tell him that they'd been happy for fifty years and ask him why would you destroy that on what may or may not have happened all those years ago? But he couldn't get it out of his mind. 'We all have our secrets and they should be left in the past,' he'd repeat. He wondered if there were other secrets between them. Why didn't she tell him when she wrongly cut the material when making some curtains and had to patch them? There was no need to make a secret of that, but she did. When found out, she claimed she hadn't told him because she knew he'd go on and on about it and keep making sarcastic comments. But he wondered what other secrets might there be and not from fifty years ago? He said he knew it shouldn't really matter but it did.

Mandy would tell you that she knew Gerry was sometimes moody, but she'd also tell you that he could be great company and fun. She remembered when she first saw him, she'd fallen for him instantly; he was lively, entertaining, and handsome in a weird sort of way. Unfortunately, he was going out with one of her friends at the time, but she had asked her to pass him on when she was finished with him. Gerry wasn't the passing over type, so it was a year or more later when their paths accidentally crossed. From thereon in they started going out together. Even in those days he would have his quiet, moody moments but that didn't detract from her liking him. In fact, she had fallen in love with him very quickly.

Gerry was becoming morose about secrets of the past. 'Come on,' we'd say to him, 'pull yourself together, fifty years on; it shouldn't matter,' He'd tell you that it was over fifty years ago when he first saw her and thought she was beautiful. She had come as a blind date for his mate with whom he had a pact that they would never go out with each other's ex-girlfriends. But there had to be an exception to every rule and when they bumped into each other many months later they started dating. Very quickly he was head over heels and three months later proposed. He wouldn't have known what he would have done had she said 'No'.

Mandy told us that Gerry's moodiness was beginning to get to her. He had started to stay up late at night and then sneak off into one of the spare bedrooms to sleep. Leastwise, she welcomed being able to get some sleep and she didn't have to listen to his snoring. She was grateful they had a cruise coming up which they had booked some months before. She said she was more than ready for a break.

Gerry's doubts grew to the point they were fixed. In his mind there were secrets but what were they? He said he didn't know Mandy anymore. Why did she have secrets? Were the dalliances she had told him about as innocent as she had made out? Were the parties she went to without him just friends being friends? Was that date with Ruth's friend all it seemed to be? Was the drive out on the moors only to admire the moon reflected in the river? Did that date with the Irish doctor go no further? What were the secrets? You'd ask him if it mattered after all this time, but he'd turn a deaf ear.

When she got back from the cruise Mandy said she'd had a sense of relief as it got under way but suspected she should have gone alone. Gerry stuck to his cabin and to his side of the double bed. He kept avoiding her. Mandy noticed he appeared to be sulking but had no idea over what. He didn't want to talk to her. It was as if he had given up on life. Mandy told me that she had ran out of patience with him and went out to enjoy everything the cruise had to offer, the food, the shore trips and the entertainment, as far as she was concerned you could bring it on. She had no intention of acquiescing to Gerry's moods, belligerence, and bad temper anymore. She had a life and intended to make the most of it.

Gerry told us that as he sat in their cabin he felt that he'd lived the life of a lie. He thought his happiness was illusionary and based around lies. He'd concluded that the trust that was the foundation of their marriage was just a misty fog. He couldn't pretend any more, he couldn't look Mandy in the eye. He didn't want to sleep with her anymore.

When Mandy turned up with Simon it came as a surprise to everyone. Including herself she would claim. She said she was lounging on the deck reading some women's magazines when he approached her. Not Gerry you understand, but a friendly, smiling chap, handsome in a craggy sort of way. She did admit that she had noticed him before out of the corner of her eye. She couldn't remember how the conversation started but before long they were having a drink together, then dinner and joining each other on the shore trips. He was thoughtful, considerate and, above all else, good company. She felt there was life in her yet.

Gerry said that for him there were no more secrets. Mandy

had stopped coming back to their cabin each night. He was grateful as he preferred to be alone, he knew that truth would out.

Now he knew that all along their marriage had just been based on a lie. The secrets were no longer in the past.

Mandy told Gerry that when the cruise was over, she wouldn't be returning home with him but going off with Simon. She told Gerry that he'd given up on life and she hadn't. She also told him she couldn't stand his moods and bad temper any longer. Life's too short. She remarked that she found it interesting that she had fallen out of love with Gerry as quickly as she had fallen in love all those years ago. She reflected that, by and large, it had been a happy life although she did have to bite her tongue and compromise at times. Until Simon came along, she had been completely faithful to Gerry although she suspected he had had his dalliances along the way. But she had turned a blind eye to them. Not so long ago she had suggested that such things shouldn't come between them and had told Gerry, 'We all have our secrets and they should be left in the past.' She said she thought she couldn't have been more straight forward than that.

And that," said Sean, "was the end of the Gerrymanders. Pity we can't say the same for gerrymandering come the election."

Chapter Five
Sweet Revenge

Sean and Ducka took a walk down the High Street after their Chinese meal. They observed what had changed with more than one sentence starting with, 'I remember when...'; Ducka suddenly stopped, he looked at Sean,

"Do you realise," he said, "we sound like a couple of old farts?"

"Heaven forbid, you're right."

As Sean looked away down the High Street, he suddenly changed the subject, "Hey look, isn't that Kipper coming out of the barbers?"

"Aye up Ron how yer doing?" Sean shouted.

"Aye grandly lad, grandly, thank you."

A short rotund man came shuffling towards them scratching the back of his head below his cheese-cutter cap. They exchanged a few pleasantries and enquired about family and mutual friends. The conversation seemed about to falter when Sean said, rather tongue in cheek,

"That's a grand head of hair you've got there."

"I'll tell thee a story about the hair on my head." Ron began. "Our Lilly gets the hump if you don't mention how good her hair looks even if she has just walked past a salon, let alone called in to have her hair done. If I don't notice it and say how good it looks and make a bit of a fuss of her then I have to give her a good listening to for the next week and a half. And if I have mine cut, she'll usually acknowledge it by saying 'Had your haircut then I see?' if I'm lucky.

Anyway, you may remember I'd grown a beard. We'd gone away for an early winter break in a caravan down at Filey. It was a bargain, got it real cheap."

"Well," butted in Sean, "I wouldn't have thought a beard would have cost you anything at all unless it was a stick on one."

"No, you silly blighter, it was the caravan that was cheap, not my beard."

"So, your beard cost you nothing then," persisted Sean with his tongue more firmly in his cheek than ever.

"No, I saved money on that. I didn't have to use a razor blade, did I?" As he said this Ron realised that Sean was taking the mickey.

"Do you want to hear my story or not?" Ron said with a slight degree of petulance.

"Sorry, Ron," said Sean with a smile on his face, "you carry on. We'd love to hear your story wouldn't we Ducka?"

Ducka grunted an agreement.

"Anyway, this beard was a bit on the itchy side. Our Lilly kept telling me off. If she wasn't telling me to stop scratching it then she was telling me to stop touching it. I could hardly blow my nose before I was in trouble. I thought to heck with this I'll shave it off. But I'd sort of got used to it and what a joy not to shave every morning. I was of two minds, so, put it off for some time. Should I do it or not? The time seemed right, but I kept finding excuses not to. Then one day I decided the time had come, I decided to do it. But not just any old way. I decided to go to one of those barbers that still shaved people using a cutthroat razor. The reason for this was that I'd had a beard many years ago when I started going out with our Lilly. She kept tugging on it, so I decided to shave it off one night. I had an old electric razor which had a sideburn trimmer on it. Well, with a puff of smoke this stupid razor gave up the ghost halfway through. The next morning, I was meeting our Lilly and we were going to visit my parents for the first time. There she was in all her finery and there I was with tufts of hair sticking out all over my face. She wasn't impressed. On top of which, it had snowed that night and wasn't my face freezing."

"A case of hair today and gone tomorrow?" queried Sean.

"Ha, ha. I tell you it wasn't just a case of a cold face," continued Ron, "it was the cold shoulder as well. Where was I up to? Going to the barbers. I strode out of the house, down the street, around the corner and down the hill. But when it came to the crunch, I thought there were just too many people about. I hate queues. Too many people and queues have stopped me doing any number of things in my life - and this was one of them.

It was awhile before I had the inclination again. This time I thought I'd have it over and done with as quickly as possible. I went to our garage, got in the car, and drove down to the bottom of the hill. It seemed nice and quiet, in fact too quiet. The place was closed, and I found myself locked out from my destiny. 'Bugger,' I mumbled. Having made the effort this was a set-back.

The third time I tried I was almost frustrated again. But I persevered and it paid off. The deed was done. But would Lilly notice.

Our life together had been a close one, a life mainly without secrets. But mind you there have been some. She once bought a new top. 'Is that a new top you have on? You look lovely in it.' I said. She told me that it had taken me over a month to notice.

She thinks I keep secrets. I protest that I don't. I can be a little quiet and don't involve myself overmuch in a lot of conversation that's not needed but that's not the same as keeping secrets. If she wants to know something all she has to do, is to ask. And when she does ask, I answer her. I don't keep secrets from her. 'But that's the problem with you,' she'll exclaim in exasperation, 'You need to know the questions to ask.'

Anyway, I've lost track again, where was I? That's right, the deed was done so I thought I'd wait and see. For once I wasn't going to offer too much information, I'd let her notice for herself.

The day was one when she volunteers at the local hospital, so she didn't come home until early afternoon. Like other such Tuesdays, I'd baked a titbit for her, usually scones or a granny loaf. This day was no exception; she rang up to let me know she was on her way so that the tea and scones were on the table as she came through the door. She went straight to the bedroom and changed out of her uniform before sitting down, opposite me, in the dining room. She munched on her scones and slurped her tea and made noises of appreciation. I told her that there was something different. She wanted to know what, but I told her she'd have to find out for herself. She glanced around the room but couldn't see anything different.

She had sat opposite me and she hadn't noticed!

After eating, we went our own ways for a while. She had become engrossed in tracing her ancestors and so was soon lost to the rest of the world in research. She was now into the eighteenth century and the search was getting harder, but she was enjoying it, uncovering the odd little dalliance here and there which had produced offspring of questionable genetics.

Later in the afternoon, we watched a television programme we liked. We sat together on the settee and from time to time held hands and commented to each other about the programme. When it was over, we went our separate ways again. I kept asking if she'd noticed what was different. She said she wanted a clue. I told her I wasn't going to give her any clues, mislead her, or tell her any bare faced lies.

And she still had no inkling.

We both fussed about together in the kitchen knocking up our dinner. As we worked, we were both a little distracted as we listened to the evening news on the television in the kitchen. When the meal was ready, we sat down to eat it sitting across from each other. We clinked our glasses before drinking a glass of shandy, to accompany our meal. After the end of the meal we cleared off the plates. I was a little more affectionate than usual and gave her a cuddle and a peck on the cheek.

And she still didn't notice!

After dinner I stuck some more stamps into my album and Lilly organised the latest selection of clippings from the newspaper. One pile for this person, that pile for another, she likes to look after other people's interests. She likes to help.

Later, we watched a DVD. We sat closely together on the settee, she with her legs draped across my lap.

I asked from time to time if she had fathomed out what was different. She looked around, but still nothing, not the slightest inkling.

And as Samuel Pepys would say, 'and so to bed'.

We read for a little while before turning off the light and settling down for the night.

I couldn't contain myself anymore, I had waited for thirty years for this opportunity. Revenge had been slow in coming but it was going to be sweet.

'You do disappoint me,' I started.

'What do you mean?' came the surprised response.

'You just take me for granted,' I said.

'No, I don't. What are you going on about?'

'You do, you just take me for granted.' I said with a feigned sob.

'Don't be so daft,' she said. 'What's got into you?'

As we lay down, I gave her a goodnight kiss.

At last the light dawned, 'You've shaved off your beard!' she declared.

I don't know why that deserved a thump and I still had to give her a good listening to for the next week and a half."

Chapter Six
The Washing Machine

Ducka asked Ron if he was retired now.

"Well, I had no choice, they closed the old works down and that was me on the scrap heap. Once you pass a certain age you're not wanted."

"Must have been hard," said Sean, "and after all those years. How do you manage?"

"Thankfully, me and Lilly are comfortable. We get by, with a bit of a pension and Lilly's mother left us her house when we lost her."

"That's a bit careless," said Sean.

"What do you mean?" asked Ron.

"Losing your mother-in-law. What did you do? Take her shopping to Darlington market on a Whit Monday and leave her behind?"

"Sean, you are a silly B, as well you know, she died," said Ron somewhat impatiently.

"Sorry," said Sean.

"But you're managing alright?" asked Ducka rephrasing Sean's earlier question.

"Cannily enough," replied Ron, "but I have to be careful what I say."

"What do you mean?" asked Ducka.

Ron started, "I know it was a daft thing to say. I know I shouldn't have said it. After so many years of marriage these sorts of things just slip out without thinking. Years of trust and honesty, and not mentioning the Lada, have led to a comfortable dialogue between me and Lilly.

I said, 'There's a few bob in the bank that we should do something about.' There it was out, before I even realised it myself. It wasn't the sort of thing you could take back or pretend you were talking about something else. Off the cuff there's not a lot that you can readily rhyme with bob in a bank and get away with it. Yob in a yank for instance just doesn't make sense. Apart from which Lilly's hearing is far too acute when it suits.

At the same time as I'd uttered those fatal words, the washing machine decided it would start leaking. Not a serious leak, you understand, just a little dribble at the side; not unlike some of the old codgers you encounter on public transport. The price of cheap travel seems to be the dry-cleaning bill!

I said to Lilly that we should go back to the manufacturers and complain and demand that it be repaired under warranty. That seemed reasonable to me. My other half gave me that painful expression she reserves for half-wits and old men who drool.

'We've had it for fifteen years, it's done its dash,' she advised in her philosophical manner. She can be very philosophical between gritted teeth, can our Lilly.

'What about that fellow who repairs things?' I had offered optimistically.

'I think that one died while waiting for his next order from you,' my beloved advised in a way that you would expect from a member of the Security Council playing the veto card at the United Nations.

'There must be someone else,' I said in as supportive a manner as I could.

I then received a litany on the economics of having a fifteen-year-old washing machine repaired. I had to take into account that you would have to pay for the technician coming, and you would have to pay for their van coming. You would then have to pay for them going to the wholesaler as they wouldn't have the necessary parts on the van for a fifteen-year-old machine. Then you would have to pay them to come back and carry out the necessary repair meanwhile having to pay for the van once again. In addition, there would be the cost of the replacement parts. They would be horrendous if not extortionate. Did I know that if you built the washing machine from replacement parts it would cost as much as replacing a whole new kitchen? And it wouldn't last two minutes, the washing machine that is, not the whole new kitchen. After fifteen years if one thing was to fail then it wouldn't be long before something else went. The repair would cost at least as much as a new washing machine, if not more. 'And anyway,' came the final rejoinder, 'you've already said we have some money in the bank.'

Lilly's normally as cautious as I am with the brass, so I had a sense I wasn't going to win this one. 'Alright,' I capitulated, 'Your decision, if you would like a new washing machine, you can have a new washing machine.'

'I'm not making that sort of decision by myself,' Lilly told me. 'We have to be in agreement because that's the way we do things,' she said, before giving me a kick.

I'm always for agreement but in this case I suspected I could become impaired by her hands around my neck that could only be relieved by gasping out my full and unequivocal agreement.

Buying it was painless, armed with the size of our current machine and the space available under the kitchen bench, nothing could have been easier. We bought a machine by the same maker as the one we had. The dimensions of the machine were just about the same. And no, we didn't want an insurance policy that the salesman saw as a prerequisite for our peace of mind. We didn't want an insurance policy that would replace a problematic new machine with anything the insurer wished to replace it with including a different and cheaper brand of the insurer's choosing. And no, we didn't want installation either. Any fool can hook up a washing machine to a couple of taps, a drain and plug it into the electric socket. By doing it ourselves we avoided a screwed-up kitchen floor, that a professional installer can achieve with such aplomb and we saved £55!

Delivery occurred as requested and shortly after 1-00pm on a Wednesday, after Lilly had provided a few wiggly lines on the delivery man's scruffy bit of paper, we found ourselves with a giant cardboard box in our kitchen, full of washing machine.

By quarter past one, certainly no later than half past, we anticipated filling the machine with the dirty clothes that had piled up since removing the old machine. We expected to press a couple of buttons after Lilly had insisted on reading the instructions which I already knew through male osmosis. Then we'd coo and ahh over the swishing and gurgling sounds of our new acquisition and pat ourselves on the back for being so clever.

The removal of the machine from the packaging went to plan. Apart from being amazed by some huge elastic bands that had held things together in transit we didn't waste too much more time. I didn't even comment on the vandalism of one of the elastic bands by Lilly who took to it with a pair of scissors in a manner reminiscent of a Viking shield maiden warming up for battle.

With all packaging removed it was time to hook it up and slide it into its space. Then the skills of the original kitchen fitters came to the fore. The cavity measured 610mm just below the benchtop, the machine measured a little over its stated size of 600mm. So why wouldn't the machine slide into the hole? Because at ground level the space measured 598mm across. The suggestion of getting out my big hammer and a crowbar to persuade the washing machine into its intended resting place was frowned upon by madam.

After further examination it was deemed possible to remove the side of a cupboard immediately to the left of the allocated space. This would allow me to trim a couple of millimetres off the shelves of the cupboard but no more. In theory this should have been sufficient and with some realigning of the cupboard doors all would be well. All I can say is the trimming of shelves whilst in situ is not the easiest nor the most dust free operation I have undertaken but with the aid of my latest toy, the multi-tool, it was eventually achieved. Success! All I needed to do was hook the washing machine up and slide it into the space.

Now I have already mentioned the skills of the kitchen fitter and once more they became evident for although the original space at ground level at the front measured 598mm across, now widened to a smattering over 600mm the gap at the back of the opening was somewhat less. The washing machine did not fully go in. Further suggestions of getting out my big hammer and a crowbar to persuade the washing machine into its intended resting place was once more frowned upon by madam even though I offered to grease the sides of the washing machine first. And so, to bed, as I reminisced about what Dicken's Mr Micawber might have said. 'A washing machine 600mm wide and a hole 601mm wide; happiness. A washing machine 600mm wide and a hole 599mm wide; misery.' Didn't know I was an educated man did you Sean?"

Sean spluttered but before he could say anything Ron continued.

"Next morning, I removed the side of the drawer unit to the right of where the washing machine was going to live. This time I was even more impressed with the kitchen fitters. A steel bracket had been secured to the side with screws, as you would expect, but the top of the bracket was secured to the wood with glue. Anyway, a repeat of what I had done to the other side took place and amidst much sawdust and many expletives the task was completed. And 'Yippee' the washing machine did fit in and we tested it through its rinse cycle without a hiccough. Now all I had to do was put the drawers back in to the right-hand unit.

Two of the drawers were as good as ever, one just needed a little gentle persuasion but would run in and out with sounds not unlike drawing your fingernails across a blackboard, and one just wouldn't fit. So, after emptying out all the contents I went down to the garage to demolish one drawer and remake it. It took some effort with everything having to be pulled apart. Suitable trimming and sanding amended the width of the drawer and subject to some subsequent adjustment to the front, it fitted fine. Lilly supervised the proceedings and was suitably impressed. 'Seeing that it is so easy,' she said, 'We'd better do the other one that sticks a bit.'

So, déjà vu.

Now when we had hooked up the washing machine the instructions recommended using a water filter on the taps that lay behind the machine. We knew we had a least one but couldn't find it. In the meantime, Lilly did just that. We agreed to put it somewhere safe with a mind to installing it the next time the washing machine was pulled out which I was hoping was going to be never. Once more I foolishly opened my mouth and said that when we do pull it out it would be a good idea to put a piece of plastic from the packaging under the feet which would make it easier to slide it in and out.

This was translated as a need to do these things instantly. So, out the washing machine came, the taps behind the machine were turned off. But why we bothered, I don't know. The filter did not fit. The plastic we had trimmed so as not to show was trimmed so well it only sat under two of the feet. The washing machine was reinstalled. Never to be pulled out again in this decade. Or so I thought.

At last the machine was filled with dirty clothes, the appropriate buttons pressed, and we stood back to coo and ahh over it. Nothing much seemed to be happening, then 'E10' flashed on the screen. Lilly, being ever so clever, as she had read the manual, knew what this meant. She looked at me. 'We've forgotten to turn the water on again!' So, you've guessed it, out it came once more and was a reminder to me never to talk about money in the bank ever again.

Ee, I'd better run fellas, I'm supposed to taking our Lilly out to pick up a sack of spuds from Lowe's farm. Mind you we don't get our eggs from him, they're cheaper at the factory."

"Good to know you're still looking after your dosh," said Sean.

"Well you have to." said Ron, "You know when we first got married, we hadn't two pennies to rub together. We had bought the house but flaming solicitors' bills and stamp duty meant we had nowt to sit on. I'd resurrected a couple of old dining chairs that had been thrown into a shed. So, I set about seeing what I could do to give us something a bit more comfortable to sit on in the lounge. I'd a few sticks and a bit of canvas and not much else. I tried drawing up some plans and looked at sticking things together this way and that way. But nowt seemed to work. Then I had a bright idea and I worked it all out. I felt pleased with myself and showed our Lilly. 'Ee, that's grand' she said, 'well done, you've just invented the deck chair.' I'll have to run lads can't spend the rest of my day chatting here."

"See you," said Sean and Ducka simultaneously.

"Good luck with your bargain hunting," added Sean.

Chapter Seven
The Visited Sin

S ean and Ducka fancied a coffee and headed towards the Post House, one of their favourite haunts when younger. As they walked along High Row towards the coffee bar, a man with a smile on his face, waved and walked towards them.

"Hello, Crud." A man, slightly younger than them, and dressed in a leather jacket beamed at Sean and Ducka. He saw that Crud wasn't recognising him. "I'm Albert, used to work at the Council."

"Deary me," said Sean, "I'd never have recognised you. Gosh, you've changed."

"You're right there. I know it's only a few miles from where I come from in the dales, but it seems like a million light years away."

"We're just off to the Post House for a coffee, do you want to come?" asked Crud.

"Aye, that'd be great," said Albert.

As they walked along Sean and Ducka automatically moved across the pavement to avoid a street beggar squatting in front of what used to be Martin's bank. Surprisingly, Albert walked up to him.

"'Ow you doing Ted?"

The unkempt bundle on the footpath shuffled uneasily but didn't take his eyes from staring at the pavement to one side of him. He mumbled something. Albert put his hand into his pocket and passed some money to Ted.

"Get some food into you, Ted, and lay off the sherry. O.K.?"

The man on the pavement waved his hand in a sort of appreciation and lifted his head slightly but not sufficiently to look Albert in the eye.

Albert re-joined Sean and Ducka as they silently headed to the café.

They'd hardly finished sprinkling the brown sugar over the top of their cappuccinos when Ducka's curiosity started the conversation.

"You know that fella on the pavement then?"

"He comes from a pit village over in the next dale from where I was born. When I was younger the village was a bustling community that thrived on its coal mine. Half a dozen rows of terraced houses nestled in the valley overshadowed by the hills of slag around them. Here and there houses had been converted into a pub, a grocer's shop, and a hardware store further down the road. It was typical of so many mining communities in the dales.

The roads were largely unmade apart from the main road that went through the centre. These unmade roads ran past the backyards of houses. The fronts were serviced by a clay footpath at the end of the garden. At the end of the village, furthest from the mine, was a row of half a dozen houses that were more substantial than the average miners' fare, these were for the more senior managers and clerks at the pit. The mine manager had a detached house surrounded by a large garden out towards the countryside.

Every Sunday, duty saw that the villagers would parade past the manager's house and on through the graveyard as they went to St. Andrew's Church. Once a week and twice at Easter and Christmas they beseeched God to take care of their masters, the village and almost as an afterthought, themselves.

Between the pit and the village was the Miners' Institute. This was a centre where you could use the library to borrow books and study to better yourself or go there to meet your mates for a pint and get drunk on a Saturday night. The bar was closed on a Sunday.

Beside the Institute was a swimming pool. Families used to throng around on warm evenings and weekends; that was until young Tommy Rawson drowned there. Now it remains empty and forlorn.

The Institute is where everyone gathered when there was an accident down the pit or there was some other local disaster.

Everyone knew everybody's business apart from what they didn't want to know. In that case they'd turn a blind eye and pass judgement in whispers.

When not working during the day the men would sit on the backyard doorstep, their faces drawn in, smoking their tabs, as their cigarettes were known. Occasionally an old timer, someone old before their time, would come shuffling and coughing his way past. Clearing his throat and spitting into the gutter, he would jaw with the younger men. The older man thinking he was like that once and the younger thinking he'd get out of the pit before silicosis got him; but turned a blind eye to the fact that there was nowhere else to go.

Ted, who you saw squatting on the pavement, is Edward, son of Derek and Joan. He was born into that community but was never really part of it. He was an only child. He and his parents lived in Victoria Terrace, in a house where downstairs there was a scullery and pantry at the back and a living cum dining and everything else room at the front. Upstairs were two bedrooms. Modern plumbing hadn't come to the village so the netty, or toilet to Derek and Joan, was an earth closet across the backyard.

Derek and Joan were honest, upright, hardworking stalwarts of the village. Derek had worked hard enough to become a deputy down the pit. This distanced himself from a lot of the other miners who tended to have some distain for upstarts. But he didn't care; he'd rather have the extra pay than be their mate. They frowned on him anyway as he and Joan didn't attend St. Andrew's as most of the village did. He and Joan went to the chapel in the next village. They were a handsome but remote couple.

Edward was given every opportunity. They discouraged him from playing with the other children as they didn't want him to be brought down to the level of the kids who lived in the area. They winced if anyone called him Ted. His name was Edward after Edward the Great, son of Alfred the Great and that's what he was going to be, great.

Edward was given no opportunity other than to work and

study hard. And that's what he did, within his abilities. Derek and Joan were disappointed when he didn't pass the exams to go to the Grammar School but hoped he might make something from his piano lessons if nothing else.

He left school when he was fifteen and to the relief of Derek and Joan was successful in getting an apprenticeship at the nearby engineering works. He didn't let them know that at work he was Ted. He continued to study and work hard and became well regarded. Because he could play the piano, he was invited by some of the lads he worked with to join a rock band. He would have liked to, but it was a bridge too far for Derek and Joan. They hadn't invested all their hard-earned money into his piano lessons for him now to waste it by playing that muck. He had to play proper music. You never know, he could be a concert pianist one day.

By the time Ted was twenty he had passed all his trade exams, he was being paid well notwithstanding he was still in the final months of his apprenticeship. And so, he found himself with money in the bank and time to spare as he no longer had to study at the kitchen table under the demanding gaze of Derek. He might have had more in the bank if he hadn't been paying a fair whack to Derek and Joan for rent. Derek had generously said that when he completed his apprenticeship then he could have the final pay packet for that week all to himself.

It was agreed he could buy a car. He could take them out for a drive on a Sunday afternoon after chapel. That would be nice.

Derek had agreed a Sunbeam Talbot would be fine, so Ted tracked one down. Joan thought the neighbours would be quite jealous seeing that parked outside their house. It wasn't the sports car Ted would have liked but it was a convertible so he could at least have the wind blowing through his hair on a fine day.

As diligently as he'd studied for his apprenticeship, he prepared for his driving test with Derek relentlessly going over the highway code with him. He took lessons as he knew no one well enough to take him out in his own car. He passed first time.

The car gave him newfound freedoms even if the Sunday afternoons became somewhat of an ordeal. His parents sat in the back seat and issued instructions to their chauffeur. 'Not too fast, if you please.' 'No, don't go that way; we wouldn't want to be seen there.' Why they wanted to park on a triangle of land at one of the country road junctions not far from the village and just sit there for hours on end, goodness alone knows.

With time that was now his own and the freedom the car gave him Ted took it on himself to join the amateur dramatics society in a nearby town. He offered to help backstage with the scenery. It was there he met Linda; she was taking one of the parts. She was pretty and well dressed. He liked her.

His experience with girls had been non-existent. He'd spent most of his life so far being compelled to study for this, that and the other, he was discouraged from going out with anyone, boy or girl. His only knowledge of girls had been what he'd heard from the chaps at the engineering works or the example of his parents. He had no sense of the reality of his workmate's bragged sexual exploits. There must have been some truth in them as most were now married. Mind you that didn't stop their comments as to what they would do to the page three model if they ever ran into one.

He'd known Linda by sight as she lived in the village. She was the daughter of the Chief Clerk at the mine and lived in one of the better houses on the edge of the village. She worked as a telephonist at the nearby County Council offices. Whilst her parents had been protective of her, she had been allowed to mix with other villagers, but they would prefer she didn't end up marrying a miner. A sea captain would be good but where was she going to find one in the middle of a pit village? Dream on. She had been flattered that a few of the local lads had tried it on from time to time. But she was equally self-confident enough to repel such advances without there being too many hard feelings.

Ted finally plucked up courage to offer to drive her home after a rehearsal. She thought him handsome enough, smartly dressed, and polite if somewhat shy. She knew through the village gossip that he'd worked hard to better himself although she understood his parents had been rather overbearing. Maybe that was why he was a little shy, but in a cute way. He was the sort of guy she'd like to know a little better.

The first time he took Linda home he shook hands with her as a way of saying goodbye. He agreed to pick her up the next week and it wasn't until the third week that she got a peck on the cheek when he said, 'goodnight.' By the fourth week there was a nervous attempt at something resembling a proper kiss.

He mentioned at work that he was going out with this girl and his workmates couldn't help their curiosity. 'What was she like?' 'Did she have big tits?' 'Had he had it away yet?' And so on. His reticence revealed his virginal state. Then the advice started. 'Feel her tits.' 'Get your hand up her skirt.' 'She'll be gagging for it.' 'Get stuck in.'

He wished he'd kept quiet.

The following week when they came to say goodbye there seemed something different, something special, something inviting in her kiss. He brushed off enquiries about her at work but thought about her all week. The next meeting couldn't come soon enough.

When Ted next picked her up for rehearsals they briefly kissed before they set off. At the rehearsals he emerged from his behind the scenes tasks to challenge one of the other players who was being rather mean to Linda about her acting. This led to some embarrassment. The people on the stage suddenly becoming noticeably quiet and avoided each other's eyes whilst pretending all was normal.

Linda thought it was nice to have someone speak up for her and try and protect her. Notwithstanding, she would have preferred to have avoided the embarrassment and the cavern that had opened between her and the other players. The goodbyes that evening, as they left rehearsals, were subdued.

As they drove home Ted started to tell Linda, in rather a clumsy way, of how much he liked her and how he would like to see her more often. Linda thought that would be nice. What she wasn't prepared for was to suddenly find Ted's left hand thrust up her skirt. She was alarmed, yelped, and leapt up as much as the car would allow, trying to get his hand away. She couldn't remember too much more apart from leaves rushing by.

Ted had felt things were going well with Linda whom he thought was giving him encouragement. He was startled and shocked at Linda's reaction; she catapulted into him causing him to lose control of the car. It lurched through a hedge and down a bank. A car passing on the other side of the road saw what had happened and quickly drove on to find the nearest phone box to alert the emergency services.

The police weren't too long in getting there and used a light on the police car to probe through the dark. They easily spotted the crash site. They couldn't believe what they saw. It looked like a woman had been thrown out of the car in the crash. She was unconscious. Her underwear was around her left ankle and lying on top of her with his trousers and underwear around his knees was a man.

When the light hit Ted he hurriedly tried to stand upright and pull up his trousers. But it wasn't only the light that hit Ted that night. A bobby, full of adrenalin fuelled anger, rushed, and tumbled down the bank. He hit Ted with such a force that Ted thought he was going to die; he couldn't get his breath. He was manhandled, kicked, and elbowed up the bank, through the hedge and pushed into the police car. It wasn't a case of mind your head getting into the car, quite the reverse, a sharp shove made sure he hit the side of his head on the edge of the car's roof.

This was the start of what he'd have to get used to for the rest of his life. The venom, the abuse, the punch, and the kick came from all directions, and often the one he wasn't looking in.

He didn't see the inside of his home again. The news of what he'd done spread quickly throughout the village and just as quickly the anonymous bricks came through the front windows of the house where he had lived in Victoria Terrace. Derek and Joan quickly let it be known that they had disowned their son and that they weren't going to let him set foot in their house ever again. Shortly after Edward was sentenced, they moved away without leaving a forwarding address.

Ted went from police cell, to prison, to court and back to prison. His deed featured in all the papers, not just the tabloids. People could not understand how he could do such a thing. Even the Judge was incredulous. His early guilty plea didn't seem to make too much difference to his sentence. He didn't find prison easy.

It wasn't only Ted who served a sentence; Linda's life had changed forever. She couldn't understand what she had done that warranted what had happened to her. The examinations and processes following the crash left her disturbed. At times it felt as if she was the guilty one and not the victim. She was relieved to find she wasn't pregnant or had any sexually transmitted disease, but that was small comfort.

She now seldom went out in the evening and never accepted a lift where she would be the sole passenger with a male driver. She no longer felt confident and stopped dating boys. The local boys knew they would be rejected and soon stopped asking her out. She had given up her job and stopped wearing makeup. Her clothes changed from being chic to frumpy. She spent a lot of time by herself in her room staring at the ceiling or the wallpaper. On a Saturday she would occasionally go for a brisk walk to the village grocery shop to buy one or two personal things. When people tried to stop her and ask her how she was she'd ignore them and hurry past. She didn't want to share her total disarray. She didn't know how to. Why her? She couldn't understand it.

Then one day she heard what she didn't want to hear. Ted was out of prison and had been seen in the village. So, his sentence was over but hers was a life sentence.

When Ted was released from jail he didn't know where else he could go but back to the village. He knew nowhere else. He went to live in a boarding house that had once been an old farmhouse in the days before the mine shaft had been sunk. It was a place where itinerants and casual farm workers bunked down as they chased their work across the seasons.

Ted went to see his old engineering firm to see if he could get a job but soon learned that if he was seen around there again then he'd soon know what for. There was no work at the mine for him; the management felt they couldn't guarantee his safety once he was out of their sight. No farmers wanted to employ him. There was no work anywhere for a man like Ted.

If he ventured into the village it was soon made clear to him that he wasn't welcome. He tried going into the Institute for a drink but was told it was for members only and not only wasn't he a member he never would be.

The grocery shop served him but with minimum civility. If there were people in the shop the conversation would stop as soon as he entered. They would say, 'Serve him first,' to get him out of the shop as quickly as possible.

Leaving jail didn't mean his sentence was over.

Once walking through the village, he heard a woman's anguished voice behind him, 'Why Ted, why?'. He scurried away not looking back, not daring to look back but with his eyes fixed on the path immediately in front of him.

He started drinking but where he got it from nobody knew. The hardware shop soon stopped selling him methylated spirits. It was thought he was getting drugs from somewhere but again nobody knew from where. At times he would be found living rough, under a hedge, in someone's allotment shed and sometimes under a bridge. Complaints were made to the police which resulted in him disappearing for a month or two. Sometimes in jail again, sometimes not. When he returned he was seldom sober. He hardly knew where he was, what day of the week it was or why he was where he was. That was how he wanted it to be.

He kept seeing the girl and the car in his mind's eye and occasionally thought he saw her in the distance but when he did, he ran away from the mirage as fast as he could. He'd hide behind whatever he could, a wall, a tree, or a hedge; he'd go and search for another bottle to help him forget.

Linda had seen Ted once or twice in the distance. Prison had altered him but living rough more so. She was once close enough to call out to him, but he had run away. Even after all those years, her anger had not abated. 'Why me? Why him? Why me?'

Sometimes Ted was soberer than at other times, which he needed to be to get served at the grocery shop. Ted's basic food was bread and cheese and any other scraps he could filch.

One day Linda saw Ted enter the grocery shop. She hurried to the door and flung it open. She saw no one else there, no one but Ted. She advanced on him, her fury more than apparent. He backed into a corner, as she advanced towards him. He cowered in a crouched position. He put his arms up around his head to protect himself.

'You scum. You filthy lousy stinking scum! You, you, you.' Linda's voice reached an unnatural pitch. She was momentarily lost for words in anger and exasperation, 'You louse! What did I do to you? What harm did I do to you? What right do you think you had to do what you did? Why did you do that to me?'

Ted did not answer but pushed himself past her, hearing Linda, in a much more measured but angrier voice asking him again, 'Why? Why did you do that to me?'

Immediately after that Ted left the village. You'll see him begging on the streets around here, or Middlesbrough and sleeping either rough or in one of the hostels for the homeless."

It sounded as if Albert had finished his tale when Sean broke in.

"Albert," he started, "forgive me saying so but it sounds like Ted deserves all he has got and more. What I can't understand is why did you give him some money? From what you've said, if I was on my way to Damascus and saw him on the other side of the road I'd cross over just to make sure he'd been given a good kicking and, if not, I'd give him my halfpennies worth as well."

"And that might be fair if that's all there was to it. And

some of the stories only started to come out long after Ted's parents had moved on. The silence of the village was its shame. So, when it was all too late, the tales emerged in a sub voce voice told behind closed doors. It was said that Ted's father, Derek, wasn't the nicest of people. He would often give his wife a good hiding but never in a way it would show. He would also force sex on her whenever he felt like it and sometimes in front of Ted. In addition, he'd abused Ted. All of which was hidden behind a code of silence which would have had dire consequences for Ted and his mother if it had been broken. One man's depravity had hurt so many people."

"I now understand why you slipped him some money," said Sean, "I hope he takes you up and buys some food with it."

"It would be nice to think so," said Albert, "but more than likely it'll go on cheap sherry or cider. That's why I don't give him too much but ask the Sallies to keep a look out for him."

Albert's girlfriend Joyce walked in and stood by their table.

"Hey, what's the long faces for, lost a bob and found a tanner?" she asked.

Joyce's presence had suddenly brightened their lives and smiles returned to their faces. It was agreed it was time for a pint at the King's Head.

Chapter Eight
Annabel

Sean, Ducka, Albert and Joyce sat around the table in the lounge of the King's Head talking of people they knew in common and laughed over Albert's bubble car when it had been the subject of more than one prank. Albert said although it was funny now, he didn't think it was at the time and thought Sean and Ducka were a pair of miserable sods. Sean and Ducka admitted they couldn't deny this. "But in retrospect," Albert said, "it was Ernie I held the biggest grudge against."

"What happened to him?" asked Sean.

"He started carrying a knife. He used to go down to York

and get involved in some of the gang fights. I heard he used to hang about on the periphery of a fight and just dart in and give someone a quick jab before backing off, typical of him. The cops got him one day and he still had his knife on him. He was sent down for a couple of years and after that he seems to have disappeared. And what about you Crud, have you come back to chase Pru again?"

"How did you know I used to go out with Pru?" queried Sean.

"If you are going to do your courting up the dales don't you think I might hear about it?"

"Sadly, that was all over when I left town. I hope she's happy and that Ken is looking after her."

"Haven't you heard? Ken was killed in an accident on one of his building sites. A bulldozer driver didn't see him and crushed him against a wall."

"That's sad news, poor Pru."

"You should look her up," said Albert.

"No, there's too much water under the bridge by now."

"Well, if you do, I think she lives somewhere in Eskdale."

"Talking of women from the dales, I hear there's one who's made a bit of a name for herself in the film world. Did you ever come across her?" asked Ducka.

"I think you're talking about Annabel. She came from way up in the dales, real six fingered territory. I don't know her but know of her. It's an interesting story."

And so, Albert began the tale of Annabel. "She was born and brought up on a remote farm. There seemed nothing to distinguish her name from those given to the few cows they had. The farm was begrudging of its fertility and placed heavy demands on whoever tried to farm it. Her mother and father had no option but to spend most of their time working to exist. They each knew the tasks they had to perform, some of it together but much of it apart. They knew the tasks by day, by week, by month, by season and by year; there was no option and little respite. Because they knew this, there was no need to talk much, indeed the years had made them more and more withdrawn.

Apart from weddings and funerals they rarely left the farm. Occasionally, they went into town on market day where they might buy or sell a cow here or a pig there. They might bump into some of their neighbours from further down the valley, pass the time of day with them and arrange to help with tasks that were bigger than they could be manage. They bought the few essentials they could afford. They frowned on the farmers who stood in the doorways of public houses with glasses of beer in their hands. If they had money like that, they wouldn't waste it the way that lot did. It was a long way into town and an even longer way home.

There had been hope, once. They started with a couple of pigs and slowly and selectively bred the numbers up so that they had a drift of seventy-nine. They had hopes of increasing still further and having a reasonable living for their efforts. Back then, there was a swagger in their step rather than the gait they now had. That was before swine vesicular struck. They weren't affected but were still ordered to kill all their pigs. When they were allowed to restock, the compensation they received bought three pigs and their dreams were buried along with the seventy-nine.

It's hard to know if Annabel was a wanted child but she wasn't unwanted and there was affection. She took her place by the fireside in the evening along with the cats and was fondled and stroked just as much. When she was old enough to wander the farm, she could do so freely while her mother and father concentrated on what needed to be done in the fields. When she grew a little older, she too had her chores. They weren't too onerous to start with, like feeding the hens, but enough to start getting her used to the ways of the farm. When she was older, she could find herself cleaning out ditches on bitterly cold days with the blisters freezing on her hands.

For all of this she was a happy person with a ready smile that people gratefully accepted as a reward. When she visited neighbours or visited town she unabashedly went around saying 'Hello' to all and sundry. She shared in people's lives, she laughed with their joys, she was sad for their losses. She helped people to cross the road, she carried their bags, she just liked people and liked being with them. She was kind to them, and they were kind to her. She was as sociable on one side of the scale as her parents were withdrawn on the other. Where this came from no one was sure, some, with a twinkle in their eye, conjectured that it might have been a passing gypsy. Others, more realistically, thought it must have come from all those radio programmes that she listened to. It was hard for anyone to say her name, Anna, or Belle never Annabel, without a smile in their voice.

She was dressed in clothes remade from her mother's cast-offs. Her mother from time to time was given well-read women's and fashion magazines. She would cut down her old clothes and remodel them as best as she could to resemble something that had caught her eye in one of the magazines. Anna would read and re-read these magazines when her mother had finished with them. There weren't too many books in the house to feast on.

Anna was home schooled through a correspondence course. There wasn't much option as they couldn't afford to send her away to a boarding school. Initially her mother helped her with her studies but surprisingly quickly Anna left her mother behind. When her mother started to falter Anna started teaching her, but the mother soon became ashamed of her own ignorance and retreated to the never-ending tasks that needed to be done around the farm. Between the books she received from the school and the lessons heard over the radio she managed to get good marks on the assignments she sent in. As she got older, she borrowed more and more books from the neighbours and from the library in the town. She even built up a small library of her own from books slipped to her under the counter by Liz, who ran the second-hand bookstore in town. Before she realised the impossibility of it, she once had the ambition to read all the books in the world. And all of this whilst still carrying out her farm chores or helping her dad repair the tractor or whatever.

As she grew into her teens her beauty became more pronounced. It wasn't the beauty of the models in the magazines she used to read. It was a more complete beauty of a total person only slightly marred by hands that reflected they hadn't been mollycoddled in perfumed hand creams. The farm suddenly found itself attracting teenage boys who came calling under a variety of pretexts, offers of help on the farm, requests to hunt around the hedgerows, 'I'm lost,' 'Would you like some apples?' 'Would Anna like to go for a ride on my motorbike?' and so on. Anna enjoyed the attention, enjoyed the friendship but was very deft at changing the subject when it looked like any young man wanted to cuddle up. There were some nice young men, some handsome young men but without exception their horizons went no further than the dale they all lived in. She knew from the magazines and the radio that there was a bigger world than this and she wished to find out more about it and about herself.

When she was nineteen, she knew the time had come. By doing odd jobs for neighbours and the like she had saved almost £500. She would have liked more, but the cautious side of her nature was exploded with a proposal, if you could call it that. She was approached by a man who was a few years older than she was. They had encountered each other from time to time and had occasionally danced together at social gatherings. Without too much of a preliminary he had announced that she should marry him. Whilst she felt flattered, she didn't have the same feelings for him as he did for her. Her smile faltered as she thanked him and said she'd let him know. For some reason, the proposal gave her a sense of suffocation. She needed to break free and start a new life. The following day she told her parents she was going to leave home and try life in the city. Their heads drooped in acceptance, and they said nothing. Her mother touched her hand but soon let it drop.

So it was that three days later Anna took advantage of a ride into town from a neighbour. Her parents didn't wave her off, they didn't know how to say goodbye; they turned their back on her and took their unexpressed sorrow into the fields. Anna's tears from leaving home were masked by the excitement of what she faced. Her stomach told her she was scared but she was full of anticipation.

She had a little time in the town before her bus left. She walked around and said goodbye to familiar places. She said goodbye to her friends and a special goodbye to Liz. Liz told her to get on with it and have a life for her as well, she'd miss her and don't forget to write. All too soon the bus was there; a final look behind her just in case her parents had come to wave her goodbye, but no, she was now on her own.

The bus drove through the night. Fellow passengers huddled into all shapes and contortions as they sought sleep and sniffed and snorted. Anna didn't feel like sleep. The shadows outside the bus matched the shadows of her mind. She wondered what she had done but equally knew she couldn't go back. The further the bus drove her away from where she had come from the more elated she felt.

It was mid-morning by the time they reached the city. As they rode downtown to the bus station, she was having difficulty taking everything in. As she looked at the buildings, the shops, the roads, the cars, the people, it was like looking through a giant kaleidoscope. When they finally came to a halt one of the passengers told her where the restrooms were. She collected her luggage, then went and spruced herself up and was ready to face the world.

She needed to find somewhere to stay until she could find a room for herself. From what she had read the best thing was to head to the nearest YWCA. She didn't know where that was but saw a bustling coffee bar not too far away. She'd ask there and maybe have a coffee first. She asked one of the waitresses behind the counter if she knew where the YWCA was. By dint of calling to another waitress across the room directions were given to Anna who then asked for a coffee. She was taken aback when asked what sort of coffee? The waitress pointed to the board hanging above her head. She asked for a cappukino and had her pronunciation corrected. She took her drink and her suitcase to a table that had just been vacated. She thought it a funny coffee, more froth than anything. Well that's the city for you she thought to herself. When she got to the liquid part of the coffee, however, she found it tasted differently from any coffee she had had. It was rather nice.

As she sat there a couple of young men came and sat at her table, one to the front and one to the side. They lent in eagerness towards her. They were bronzed, tattooed, full of smiles and dressed alike in white T-shirts, Levis and Nike sneakers. Art and RC introduced themselves. Anna was told RC's initials were

RC, but he was also called that as some woman had commented on his beautiful tight backside. Despite thinking they were a bit forward Anna couldn't help but smile at this. She presumed Art came from Arthur. It wasn't long before Art brought the conversation around to the YWCA having overheard the directions she had received. 'Wasn't she staying in the city for long? Why would she want to go to a place like the YWCA?' She told them of her plans and of the need to have somewhere to stay while she looked around. Art looked at RC and asked if they should. RC looked doubtful and said he wasn't so sure. Art told him to come off it she was a new girl in the city needing a hand. After further negotiation RC rather reluctantly said 'alright then'. Art looked at Anna and told her it was her lucky day. They had a flat they were letting and notwithstanding that it was half promised to someone else they would let Anna have it because they liked her. But she'd have to make her mind up quick as flats like this didn't stay on the market too long. Anna was unsure, and she didn't want to see someone on the street because the promise had been broken. She was given every assurance that this wouldn't happen. Look their car was just around the corner. She could come with them, see the flat and if she didn't like it, they would drive her to the YWCA. You couldn't say fairer than that.

A couple of miles out of the city they drove into a suburb that had seen smarter days in the past. It was a little tired looking but not scruffy and it didn't feel hostile. It was a mixture of houses, some dating back to the turn of the 20th century, some more fifties in style and interlaced into this fabric were two and three storey blocks of flats built where older houses had once stood. Anna noticed an attractive parade of one storey shops on one of the streets which seemed to have a comforting neighbourly mix of stores from grocery to greengrocery and

hardware to hairdressers. Mature trees lined the streets and
flourished in gardens. She felt good about what she saw.

They pulled up to a large older looking house. She guessed
from the letterboxes that it had been divided into four flats. Art
helped her out of the car and guided her through the front door
and up the stairs to a one-bedroomed flat. RC followed. He'd
promised to lock the car so that her luggage was safe. The inside
of the flat was certainly in need of a good tidy, in fact the place
was decidedly filthy but nothing a good clean wouldn't fix.
There was a bathroom, a kitchen, a bedroom, and a lounge cum
dining room. This room was at the front of the house and had
a lovely view looking through trees and down the street. There
wasn't much furniture, a couple of single mattresses on the floor
in the bedroom, a coffee table, and some scatter cushions. There
were a few dirty pots and pans in the sink in the kitchen and
clothes strewn all over the place but mainly in the bedroom.
While she looked around the rooms Art and RC were having
hasty whispered conversations away from her.

Anna liked what she saw and knew she could make
something of the place. She asked how much it would be. Art
told her it would be £150 a week. Anna thought she could
manage that once she had a job and she had a few savings to
get her started. Art then told her that she'd have to pay a bond,
repayable of course when she moved out. It was the equivalent
of four week's rent. Anna's face fell. She said she didn't know
there was such a thing and told them how much she had in her
wallet after paying for her bus fare. RC spoke to Art in rather
an annoyed way and told him they were wasting their time.
Why didn't they just let it to the people they had promised it
to? Art persisted and said they should help Anna. He suggested
that rather than charge a bond of £600 that they reduce this to
£250 providing Anna undertook to give the place a thoroughly

good clean and then paint some of the walls when she had a
job and could afford it. RC was still unsure. Art persisted that
it was a fair deal as they would have to find the money to do
all that themselves if they let the other people have it and it
would take a couple of weeks before they'd start getting rent
again. Art said that Anna could move in straight away. RC
finally agreed. Anna was very tempted but wasn't sure if she had
enough money left for food and for travelling around the city
to find a job. Art said to help her they would throw in a bike as
well. She'd find it propped against the fence at the back of the
garden. With this assurance Anna handed over £400 and Art
handed over some keys.

Art and RC helped Anna clean up by putting all the
clothes littered about the place into polythene bags telling Anna
they'd take them off to the charity shop. They brought Anna's
luggage in, wished her the best and told her they'd call around
the following week for the next week's rent. With smiles all
around Anna waved them on their way. She was on her own.
She thought how lucky she was.

Anna could find no cleaning powders or detergents so
decided that the first thing she'd do was walk to the shops she'd
seen and stock up, she'd also get some basics to live off like
cheese, apples and bread. As she walked past the house next
door, she noticed a man sat on a rocking chair by his front
door having a coffee. She introduced herself and said she'd just
moved in. The man was pleased to hear it as the last tenants
were very noisy and played loud music well into the night. He
was John; he welcomed her to the neighbourhood and said to
ask if there was anything he could do to help.

Anna spent the rest of the day cleaning the flat, she knew it
would take a lot more to get it as she wanted but it was a good
start. Tomorrow she'd dig out the bike and start her job search.

She didn't know what sort of job she wanted but she did know what she didn't want. She didn't want to be behind the counter at a fast food joint. She settled down for the night on the floor, snuggled in the sleeping bag she'd brought with her. She didn't quite trust those mattresses until they were at least disinfected.

In the morning she went looking for the bike which she found where Art had told her. It was a man's bike but that didn't worry her. It was as neglected as the flat had been filthy. Using rags from some old clothes that Art and RC had left behind she started to clean it up. It wasn't too bad. It was a racing bike which had dropped down handlebars, but someone had turned them through 180 degrees, so they looked more like cow horns. They hadn't changed the brake levers, so they were left in an awkward position to use. One of the tyres was as flat as a pancake. She saw John was on his rocking chair and told him what she was doing and wondered if he had any spanners so she could change the handlebars and adjust the seat. John thought he had something and came back with spanners, an old bike pump, puncture repair outfit and even a rain cape all with a leather strap around them. He explained that when he was a cyclist, he would strap this bundle of necessities behind his seat tube whenever he went off. She was welcome to them as his cycling days were over. Anna quickly had the bike roadworthy once she'd bought some inner tube solution from the hardware store to repair the puncture. She got changed so that she could go out and start her search for a job. She was just about to set off when John flagged her down. He thought it would be wise if she used this tumbler lock and chain to secure her bike when she had to leave it anywhere.

And so, her job hunt began. Not having a telephone was a problem and she thought that applying for jobs through advertisements in the newspaper would take far too long.

Therefore, she resolved to find an area where there seemed plenty of businesses and go knocking on the doors. At the end of the first day she was a little dispirited. Some people had been friendly and some even suggested other places she could try, some had said they'd get back to her, but their eyes said otherwise, and some were just downright hostile commanding her to shut the door on the way out. It was a relief to share her day's disappointments with John that evening as she accepted his invitation to a cup of coffee. Just sitting down with him allowed her to stop the disappointments of the day flowing into the next. John suggested some areas of the city that may be better than others.

After a good night's sleep, she set off for another day of searching. Once again there was no luck and once more John's coffee was a comfort to her. She felt a bit more down than the first day but picked herself up again.

The third day was a repeat of the first two. She was beginning to wonder if she had done the right thing but talking to John and a cup of his coffee saw her back on track, or so she thought. That night, after seeing John, she went back to her flat. She was busy preparing some food for herself when she heard a key in the door. A man walked in; simultaneously they asked the same question each wanting to know who the other one was. The man explained that he owned the place and rented it out. Anna told her story. She told him about her dealings with Arthur. 'Arthur?' the man queried. 'Well he called himself Art.' The man hit his forehead with his hand. 'Not Arthur. Art was short for his nickname, the Artful Dodger.' The man had told Art and RC to leave for a variety of reasons including not paying the rent. He wondered if Anna knew what had happened to all the furniture, but she explained that there was nothing more in the place when she arrived over and above what he could see.

The man introduced himself as Jeff. He was sorry to tell Anna that she had been conned. He could see that she had put in some effort to tidy the place up so told her she could stay there for another 2 or at the most 3 nights but then he was sorry, but she'd have to go. She accepted what Jeff had to say but was dumbstruck. She didn't sleep much that night. She couldn't afford to stay in the city; she couldn't afford to go home; indeed, she didn't want to go home. But above all else she couldn't believe that anybody like Art and RC could be so mean and horrid. She hoped the new day would bring her luck, she needed it.

She had to give herself a good talking to before she started the day. As she was going out, she saw John. She told him all that had happened and had difficulty supressing a tear. He was furious about those 'good for nothings.' He promised that if they ever showed their faces around there again, they'd have a brick through their windscreen. Anna told him that he was not to get into trouble on her account. He said he wouldn't. He told her he didn't want to see her on the street so, if all else failed, she was welcome to stay with him until she sorted herself out. He thought she should be with young people, so it wouldn't be right for her to stay with him for too long, but she was welcome. She gave him a hug and thanked him and said she'd come and stay with him if she hadn't found anything by the time she had to leave the flat. It put her in a better frame of mind for facing the rebuttals she knew she'd find but as she said it would only take one job.

That day yielded nothing and neither did the one following. She packed her bits of pieces knowing she'd have to move out after one more night. John continued to encourage her.

Another day of trying lay ahead. She cycled to another part of the city, just off the centre, to try her luck again. She was busy locking her bike into a cycle rack when she noticed a middle-aged man looking at her. He'd just parked his bike and was dressed in lycra. She couldn't decide if he was a poser or a serious cyclist. He apologised for staring but said he was taken by the bike she was riding. He introduced himself as Al. Did she mind if he looked at it? Anna's muscles started to tighten in her stomach. This wasn't another one of Art's ruses was it? Surely the bike hadn't been stolen on top of everything else.

She let the cyclist have a look. He rode classic bikes in rallies and was impressed with what he saw. He said it was a Colnago Master, a classic and desirable Italian bike and asked her if she would like to sell it. She explained that she needed it to find a job. He'd be happy to trade in an older mountain bike and give her a couple of hundred pounds or more on top. She said that would be nice as she needed some money right now but had concerns that it may have been stolen. She gave him a potted history of what had happened to her since coming to the city. He noticed that she was wearing home-made clothes. He wove this into the conversation, and she told him a little of her background and it soon became evident she had an encyclopaedic knowledge of clothing garnered from her mother's women's magazines. Although she didn't know it, she was having a job interview on the pavement. At the end, he told her he had started a company that was still quite small. It sourced period costumes and bric-a-brac for film makers. He was thinking of taking on an intern, it wouldn't pay much but would be enough to live on; she'd be on a 90-day trial to start with. Was she interested and could she start right away?

The first task she was given was to ring the police armed with the frame number of the bike. It hadn't been reported stolen. Al did some further research of his own, went back to inspect the bike again and early in the afternoon handed her a cheque for £800. As the bike still had all its original equipment, he was happy to pay that. So that day she was taken to the bank across the street to open her first bank account.

She returned to the flat for the last night she would be there and was met by Jeff, the landlord. He was sorry he could not let her stay there any longer, but he did own a 3-bedroom flat around the corner. Three girls lived there but for family reasons one of them had suddenly to return home. He urged her to hurry round and talk to the remaining girls. She moved in the next day.

Sometimes when she was sat around with friends the subject of her childhood came up. She'd find that people imagined that being raised in such a wonderful picturesque countryside would have been idyllic. They frequently wondered if she would love to move from the city back there. She pointed out that the idyll had to be tempered with snow above the windows in winter and droughts with no water in the tanks in summer. She was not in the least tempted to go back there to live; only to visit.

She stayed with Al's firm and you will find her friends staying longer than most at the end of one of 'her' films. Two thirds of the way through the credits after the interminable producers, directors, actors, and stunts-people you may find reference to 'her' firm, Vintage Vests and sometimes you will notice Anna Belle, with a space in between. Never Annabel in full; after all she was only ever called that when she was in trouble."

"One more for the road?" enquired Sean at the end of the story.

"Why not?" replied Ducka, "It may be a canny few years before we all sit around together again."

Chapter Nine

Biggles

It was Joyce who first noticed him, he was sat by himself with a pint in front of him.

"There's Billy, he was the accountant where I used to work. I'll just go and say 'Hello', he's a lovely chap."

"Invite him over," said Albert, "the more the merrier."

Billy brightened up when Joyce spoke to him and readily came over to join them. It was nice to have a bit of company.

"Joyce says you're an accountant," said Ducka by way of opening a conversation.

"I wasn't always," replied Billy. "I started to train as one but

when I was old enough, I joined the Air Force to train as a
pilot. That was towards the end of the War. Anyway, before my
training was completed, the War ended."

"So, you went back on civvy street?" enquired Ducka.

"No, it was a canny few years before I came back to civvy
street and finished my training as an accountant. I only did
that because I found out that I could still be credited with the
studies I had passed before I joined up. It was either that or
bricklaying!"

"Bricklaying?" queried Sean, "That's a bit different from being
an accountant."

"In those days, I don't know if it happens now, when we were
demobbed, we were given a course in bricklaying, carpentry
and goodness knows what else."

"How long were you in then?" asked Sean.

"Thirty odd years," said Billy, "I loved flying."

"I take it you were able to stay on after the war and complete
your training."

"Not immediately, when the war was over, I was sent up to
Japan as part of the occupation force. I was posted around
Hiroshima. That was a sight for sore eyes. Horrible though
it was I'd rather we had that than the thought of the tens of
thousands that would have died had we had to invade. War
can be horrible." Billy poised for a moment in a quiet reflection. "I once had a Squadron Leader who had to drop depth
charges on our own people. The Italians had got a submarine
or two through the nets into Alexandria harbour and had
caused some damage to our ships. Several of our lads were in
the water. Notwithstanding, the Squadron Leader had to go
and drop depth charges in the middle of them to try and get
the subs, not the best."

"I don't know if I could do something like that," said Joyce.

"You have no choice," retorted Billy, "if you didn't take action then even more of our lads could have been killed."

"I can understand what you mean," said Joyce, "but, it can't have been easy."

"So, what sort of aircraft did you fly?" asked Ducka by way of changing the direction of the conversation.

"All sorts over the years, Hornets, Vampires, Meteors, Hunters, Bristol Freighters, VC10s; you name it and I have flown it. Mind you I started off on a Tiger Moth, that's what you were trained on."

"What's a Hornet?" asked Sean. "I've never heard of them."

"They were a bit like a De Havilland Mosquito, made of plywood with twin engines. A lovely aircraft but a bit of a handful to get in the air. Both engines rotated in the same direction, so they tended to slew to one side if you let them. They also had one other bad habit. The machine guns were just below your feet and attached to wooden batons as it was a wooden plane. When you fired those things, the recoil could dislodge the baton and then the guns could be firing in every direction. You felt lucky to survive and not have a bullet up your jacksie."

"It sounds like you were lucky to be able to tell the tale," said Sean.

"Of my echelon and the one that followed, more were killed in accidents than survived," replied Billy.

"Goodness, really," said Sean, "did you have any accidents yourself?"

"I crashed once and almost crashed twice" said Billy.

"And that didn't put you off flying?" enquired Ducka.

"No, I loved it. I took a sideways promotion from Wing Commander to Flight Sergeant to be able to continue flying. I was what the Kiwis, the New Zealanders, used to call a good bush pilot. I didn't want to be grounded and fly a mahogany desk, I wanted to stay in the air."

"So, what happened with your accidents?" asked Ducka.

"The first one happened when I went out on an exercise. The weather was a bit iffy and the fog rolled in as I was returning to base and I was diverted to another. Lo and behold that was closed before I got there due to the fog and so I was sent to a third base. I told the air traffic control to get me down quickly as I was low on fuel. Thankfully, they cleared the way. I found the approach lights and put the plane down, but once I was on the ground, I didn't have enough fuel to get the plane clear of the runway."

"Sounds like a lucky escape," said Sean.

"The next one was just as lucky," said Billy, "I was in Malaya because of the troubles. I loved the place, that's where I met my wife. She was a WRAF in the north of the country and I was down south. The RAF used to let me borrow a plane to go and visit her at weekends, for reasons best known to them, they wanted to clock up the flying hours. It suited me. Anyway, as I was saying, our squadron had started to lose some of our aircraft for inexplicable reasons. They took off, flew out as normal, radio contact was lost, and they ended up crashing. Well, one day, I went out on patrol, and everything was normal. I hadn't been in the air too long when I started to feel a little bit lightheaded. I realised something wasn't right and so headed back to base. In the control tower they equally recognised that something was wrong as I started to mutter complete and utter gibberish over the airwaves. How I managed to land the plane, I don't know, but I did. I was found in the middle of the runway, sat in the pilot's seat as high as a kite and singing my heart out. The enquiry found that one of the technicians had changed the flux he was using to repair the airlines to the oxygen mask, the flux was toxic. He was subsequently court martialled."

"Sounds like a charmed life to me," said Sean.

"Too true," said Billy, "too true."

"What happened when you really crashed?" asked Sean.

"I was at a base in Libya and had gone out on patrol late one afternoon with a navigator on board. Mid-flight the engine failed. Luck was with me and I was able to crash land on a reasonably flattish piece of desert. Following standard procedure, we sat there waiting for the recovery squad to come and get us. After some time, it became evident we were on our own. As the evening drew in, and it did so pretty fast, we could see the lights of a town and decided that as we weren't going to be rescued, we'd better walk towards it. When we got there, we rang up the base and they came and picked us up.

Once back at the base, the Base Commander had been summoned from a dinner party he was attending with his wife. He was not overly pleased to have had his socialising disturbed. 'What's the meaning of all this?' he wanted to know and before we could say anything, he continued. 'It's obviously pilot error' and then he stormed out to resume his dinner.

And that was one of the other reasons why I never wanted to fly a desk. Imagine having to deal with prats like that on a day to day basis."

"Surely, they weren't all as bad as that?" asked Albert, who had sat mesmerised throughout.

"Too many were, but folk like Rocky, that Squadron Leader I was talking about, made the difference. He was a true Biggles. He was flying a shipment of gold in a flying boat during the war when he was attacked by German fighters. He acquitted himself well and one of the Germans was severely damaged but so was his plane. He was able to land it just off the coast and scuttled it so that the gold didn't fall into enemy hands. He and his crew swam ashore to be taken prisoner by the Italians. Exactly how, I am not sure, but he turned the tables and marched close to 100 Italians into captivity. We did ask what happened to the gold. He told us it was never found but the fishing village overlooking where this all happened became mysteriously rich after the war. He made up for the prats."

"Billy, it sounds like you haven't done too badly in the Biggles stake yourself," said Sean.

With the glasses emptied, phone numbers and addresses exchanged, Albert, Joyce and Billy left Sean and Ducka to say their goodbyes.

"It just seems like we picked up where we left off," said Ducka.

"It does that," said Sean, "'til the next time. And let's hope it's not so long."

With that they shook hands and prepared to re-enter the lives they had made for themselves.

Chapter Ten
Back to the Beginning

S ean and Ducka having shaken hands and said goodbye to each other still seemed reluctant to walk away.

"Fancy a final one at the Mucky Duck?" asked Ducka referring to the Black Swan Hotel, "We can say 'Hello' to Tom and Jessie."

"Tom and Jessie are no longer there," said Sean, "I ran into Jessie the other day. She and Tom are renting a place in Cobden Street, just around the corner from where they lived when they were first married."

"Goodness gracious, really? You'll have to tell me what happened."

"Come on then," said Sean, "back into the King's Head for a final, final pint."

They settled at a table and Sean started to tell Ducka all about Tom and Jessie.

"You may remember," Sean commenced, "Tom and Jessie were a lovely couple. Everybody said so. She was as pretty as he was handsome and they both had an easy-going temperament coupled with such a wonderful smiley disposition. They were the sort of couple that you couldn't even feel jealous about but wished them well and begrudged them nothing.

They'd met at a youth club before they'd quite made their teens and soon became friends and have remained as a couple ever since. Their wedding when it came wasn't unexpected. It was a considered affair, not over lavish but all and sundry turned up to witness it. As they emerged from their local church as man and wife the crowd gushed with their 'oohs and aahs' as they liberally sprinkled rice and confetti over them.

They were a good clean-living couple who took pride in their appearance with a conservative rather than adventurous taste in clothes, he in his sports jacket and twills and her in her Jaeger style dresses. It would be true to say they weren't the sharpest knives in the drawer, they weren't University material but on the other hand neither were they stupid. She was a bank teller and he was a clerk at one of the local engineering firms.

They'd saved their money and with help of the bank that Jessie worked for they'd bought a terraced house in Harris Street. They would have liked children, ideally a boy and a girl, but not quite yet. Tom didn't earn enough to support them both. They wanted to be in a financially stronger position before they started a family. They thought they might like to have their own business but weren't quite sure what and how they could afford it. Jessie ran a catalogue business but collecting the money due was far harder than she imagined. She didn't make much for all her efforts.

They were happy with life and with each other and almost felt ungrateful that they should want something else, something a bit more, not a lot more you understand, they weren't greedy, but a bit more. They kept thinking of a nice little business of their own, something that would give them a comfortable life.

Change came on a windy, wet, miserable day. It fluttered through the letterbox in the front door and landed almost apologetically on the coir mat. And there it remained for a while before being picked up and like all other official looking envelopes was placed in a letter rack on the sideboard where all the bills were put before being opened and looked at, usually once a week on a Thursday. Only this one, when it was opened, was from, as they said, 'Uncle Ernie'. As you may recall Ernie stands for Electronic Random Number Indicator Equipment. They had held a few Premium Bonds for a little while which gave out prizes rather than pay regular interest, a sort of lottery. And they had just won a prize, not one of the £25 ones either, but a substantial one. Exactly how much, I don't know. They never said," added in Sean before continuing.

"Once they got over the shock and delight of their win they discussed what they would do with their winnings. A car maybe, a new kitchen and bathroom, a new house in a better area like the West End? They were so excited that it was hard for them to decide. Then they hit on the idea of buying a business, they'd always said they'd like a business. But what sort of business?

It was no good getting anything where technical knowledge was required as neither of them had a technical background so things like garages, plumbing, electrical repair shops were all out of the question. They discounted corner shops as they were slowly but surely being put out of business by supermarkets. Although an off-licence selling wine, beer and spirits was a possibility. The idea of a coffee bar was quickly forgotten when they thought of having to deal with unruly mods and rockers, but maybe a restaurant, that had merit, after all Jessie liked cooking.

A simultaneous light shone between them. 'What about a pub?' said one, 'With grub,' said the other. They agreed a pub with grub was the way to go. They were sociable, they liked people, the more they thought about it the more it seemed exactly right for them. They felt excited and wondered the best way to go about it. A visit to their local pub, that's what was called for.

It was quiet in the Copper Beech, so Ian, the publican, was only too happy to join them at their table and give them some advice. As they were new to the trade with no previous experience he suggested looking at a tenancy that was tied to a brewery, with that they'd get brewery support and training and get a better margin on the beer they sold. As opposed to having what was known as a free house where they could have more than one brewery supply them, but they were largely on their own for support. The downside of the tenancy was that the brewery's interests came first, it was all about the gallonage, the amount of beer they could sell. Any other interest they might have such as accommodation or catering had to be woven around the sale of ale.

After going home and thinking about it further they

decided to go down the tenancy route, apart from which tenancies were cheaper to get into. Ian gave them an introduction to the brewery who he said were as good as most and better than some. They put in an application and were soon given an interview.

The interview quickly turned from one where they stressed their sociability and expressed their desire to become 'mine host' into one of did they realise the hard work it took to become a good publican? How well equipped were they to deal with hiring and managing cleaners and bar staff, what skills did they have to account for the money and make sure it was all accounted for and make sure all bills were paid on time? What about managing stock, stock rotation, stock taking, stock ordering? What did they know about pulling a good pint, how could they make sure the beer being served was in prime condition? There were more points made about ensuring pipes were kept clean, indeed a whole series of things about hygiene and cleanliness. And did they realise the hours they would be committed to, seven days a week. There was far more to it than just greeting customers and smiling, as important as that may be. They had to realise it was a commitment and it was hard work. It would be a business they were running.

They were accepted by the brewery and soon found themselves on a training course that taught them all the necessary basics of running a public house. They were then sent to a tied house, a pub owned and run under management for the benefit of the brewery. Here they were put to work in all aspects of the business from cleaning the toilets in the morning to clearing up the tables and bar last thing at night. It was exhausting but satisfying.

Their reward was to be offered a small public house in a

side street near the centre of town, The George. Other hostelries around and about were thriving but this one was down at heel. It had been popular, but through the last two tenants the place had run down. They could really make something of this and build it up again. If they did it right the brewery promised them they'd be in line for bigger premises, but they needed to prove themselves first.

A couple of days later saw them taking stock at The George, all they'd have to pay for was the stock and a few fixtures and fittings. A quick negotiation was helped by the outgoing publican wanting out in double quick time, he'd had enough. And lo and behold the licensee's shingle with Tom's name on it was hung above the door, the place was theirs.

The George consisted of one bar servicing an L-shaped lounge, upstairs was a private sitting room, kitchen, and bedroom. Downstairs there was a cellar where the beer kegs were kept. The whole place was filthy, so Jessie set to and cleaned the place up with copious amounts of soap and water starting in the public area before moving upstairs. Tom, in the meantime, concentrated on the beer pipes, pumps and all around the bar including the long-neglected drip trays and spirit dispensers. Carpet cleaners were called in. In short order the place was spick and span and a sandwich board was placed on the pavement to advertise The George's new management.

Business was slow to begin with and the street people dropping in just to use the toilet were obviously turning off the few people who were coming in for a drink. Tom didn't like to do it, but he had no choice if they were to make a go of it. He barred the homeless people. One turned quite nasty, so Tom had to grab hold of him and physically throw him out. He returned to the bar to find the few in the pub applauding him and offering to buy him a drink. On the one hand he felt satisfied, on the other hand he didn't sleep well that night as he kept going over the events of the day. Jessie told him to forget it, he had no choice, but Tom didn't like confrontation and the thoughts stayed with him for a few more days.

News seemed to have got about and The George started to become busier. Requests for something to eat resulted in more than a packet of crisps or nuts being offered for sale. Jessie starting to make sandwiches, nice ones, not just cheese and ham, but smoked salmon, game pâté, and the like which were put into a brand-new sandwich cabinet kept on the top of the bar. She prepared jars of pickled eggs, then scotch eggs and before long she was offering a ploughman's lunch. Finally, they offered pie and peas in a bowl. They recognised they couldn't go any further as their kitchen upstairs was small and there was only so much they could cram on the bar and its surrounds.

Their popularity and that of The George grew and with it they were making a comfortable living helped somewhat by advice they'd received from people who'd been in the trade a long time. They kept a separate till for their food and made sure that not all sales were recorded, easy when the till was already open for another transaction or the drawer not fully closed. It was placed low enough behind the counter for patrons not to notice, not that they would care anyway, but just in case there happened to be someone from Inland Revenue on the other side of the bar.

Tom grew with the trade and became more gregarious than he naturally was. When customers offered 'one for yourself,' Jessie would thank them, take their money, and put it in a glass below the bar. She would toast them with a half pint glass of Coca-Cola, and she would keep on serving, clearing the tables, or doing whatever was needed. On the other hand, when it wasn't too busy and he could see Jessie could cope, Tom would accept the offer of 'one for yourself' by pouring himself a drink and going and joining the customers at their table. It helped the popularity of both Tom and The George. When Jessie thought the workload was getting a bit disproportionate Tom explained that all she had to do was call and ask and to realise that he was working too, by keeping the customers happy.

Tom looked after the morning beer deliveries. When all the empty casks were on the lorry and full ones safely stored in the cellar he'd sit down with the draymen and have a glass of beer. He explained to Jessie he had to demonstrate that they took good care of their beer and pulled a good pint at The George. He was sure it did no harm for this to get back to the Brewery. Jessie felt a little more reserved about it but knew the draymen expected a drink.

The George was a big commitment on their time and only one or the other could manage to take a break when it wasn't too busy, they couldn't both go out at the same time. To make amends for this they occasionally invited some of the customers, who they'd got to know, to stay behind after closing time and join them for a relaxing glass or two at a table that was out of sight of the windows. There was one rule, there were no free drinks, they all had to be paid for and the money put into the till, even when it was Tom's and Jessie's round. This kept the books straight.

Tom turned the occasional invite into a regular affair. At times Jessie was too tired to hang about for too long so after a glass she would leave Tom and his new friends to it and retire to bed. His state of grogginess the following morning would tell her how long the session had lasted.

The Brewery were pleased how the couple had built up the business and called them to a meeting after they'd been at The George for 18 months or so. Through the flattery, the gist of the conversation was that they wanted them to purchase the tenancy of a much bigger premises in the suburbs. It had seen better days, but the Brewery was sure Tom and Jessie could turn it around the way they had turned around The George. They said that the potential gallonage was 5 times greater than where they were, and it had a commercial kitchen. They advised they had a buyer for The George who was prepared to offer a good price. In addition, the Brewery's finance arm would give them some support. Over a generous lunch Tom's enthusiasm increased with each glass of wine he drank. The meeting ended after the coffee liqueurs had been drunk and Jessie and Tom were asked to think about it over the next couple of days and come back to them. Tom said there was no thinking about it, but Jessie interjected a word of caution saying that of course they'd want to see the books first.

So it was that three months later Tom and Jessie took over the Black Swan known by one and all as the Mucky Duck. It was a far different business to run than The George. Staff were needed for the bars, for cleaning and for cooking and not everyone wanted to put in an honest day's work. Early on Tom found that cigarettes were going missing from one of the bars. He set up a trap and caught one of the barmaids. He was taken aback when all she could say in defence was, 'you can afford it.'

The other big problem they found was that one of the reasons for the decline in the popularity of the pub was that a disreputable gang of men had become regulars there. They were big drinkers and as their beer went down so their aggression went up. Consequently, they were frightening away many. Tom wasn't sure how he could tackle this. It wasn't like dealing with the few homeless people he had moved on from The George. He also knew that even if he could get rid of them there would be a lull in income before he could start attracting people back again. When talking to the Brewery about it they thought he should just front up to the gang and tell them they weren't wanted. Tom didn't think they were the sort of people who'd react well to such an invitation.

The solution came one day when he voiced his frustration to Kev, one of the regulars he had got to know through him popping in for a pint after work. Kev told him he knew a couple of the gang members and maybe it could be arranged for them to go elsewhere but, like most things, it would have a price. He told Tom about the time the gang had once bought a penthouse in a new development. The developer didn't know he'd sold to gang members until it was too late. Once the news leaked out nobody wanted to buy the remaining apartments. The developer ended up buying the penthouse back at a much-inflated price. So, if Tom wanted Kev to talk to the gang he was happy to do so. Tom gave the go ahead. When he told Jessie about it she just hoped that they weren't going to end up buying even more trouble.

A few days later agreement was reached. The gang had its own clubhouse. Tom was to supply it with beer and spirits at cost, settlement on 20th of the month following. This was better credit than the brewery gave him, but he felt he had no choice and would have to live with it. A sum of money, in used notes, was also to be handed over.

The last night the gang was there was a rowdy affair and their final hurrah was a couple of bricks through the Mucky Duck's windows. Tom found it all very unsettling and he needed more than a couple of stiff drinks before retiring for the night. He just hoped he'd done the right thing and that that was the end of them.

The sandwich boards went out advising passers-by that the Black Swan was under new management. Another advised that the menus had been revised with meal specials every day. Events were put on, quiz nights, darts tournaments and at the weekends they had jazz. They didn't want pop groups as that would draw in a crowd which could be as bad as the gang they'd got rid of.

Bit by hardworking bit they built the trade back up. Tom concentrated on the front of the house and Jessie on all the paperwork, the ordering, paying the bills, paying the staff whilst keeping a close eye on the restaurant side of the business. Both pitched in as needed when they were very busy.

As they started to build up their popularity they had a visit from a couple of the gang members who used to frequent the place. They offered their protection services. There was no choice but to pay if they didn't want their trade disrupted. It was cash straight out of the till.

Tom and Jessie were making a go of it but weren't finding life as much fun as when they were at The George. Tom was drinking a lot more with the patrons. Jessie from time to time caught him taking a glass of beer not long after breakfast. His excuse was that he was just checking to see the quality was alright. He was also socialising after hours with a select group in a back bar. The discipline of making sure all drinks were paid for slowly broke down to the point where his 'friends' were helping themselves without too much regard to paying full price if indeed anything at all.

Tom began to wonder where the light was at the end

of the tunnel. He and Jessie were drifting further apart, with each looking after their separate responsibilities. It was seldom that Jessie joined him and his cronies for a glass after the close of business. He needed a drink to wind down at the end of the day, some days more than others. It was he who ended up evicting the drug dealers or dealing with the increasing demands for protection money. The gang were taking their 'fee' by not paying for the booze that had been supplied to them. Some days he wondered how they'd ever get out of this situation. He felt trapped in many ways including, being in-hock to the Brewery. What they needed was a nice little pub in the country that did a bit of bed and breakfast, that would be nice. He couldn't carry on like this, he had to do something about it.

Initially it was just a few quid from the till, and he was successful enough to start to build up a nest egg and put the money back. He thought he'd venture a bit more but, a dead cert for the 3.30 at Catterick would have been better used if it had been put in the shafts of a milk float. Soon he was betting more to try and cover his losses. To finance his betting, he was selling off some of the stock at bargain prices from the back door of the Mucky Duck. He was keeping this secret from Jessie. He wanted to give her a lovely surprise one day when he'd had a big win. He was looking forward to seeing that smile on her face when he told her they were getting out and buying a country pub, somewhere peaceful, quiet, and friendly. Meanwhile the stress of it all meant he drank more and more.

When Jessie got her surprise, it was on a Sunday evening and it wasn't the one Tom had planned. He had run out of excuses for money not balancing and stock being mislaid, on top of which he owed the bookies a reasonable amount. Jessie felt betrayed in a way she'd never experienced before. She told

Tom to get out of her sight, they'd talk about it tomorrow and if he had thoughts of going downstairs to have a drink he'd better think again. She spoke in such a measured chilling way that Tom knew if there was to be a tomorrow for them he wasn't going to have a drink that night. He slunk off to the guest bedroom feeling utterly devastated at the pain he'd caused Jessie.

The next day, with her private tears behind her, Jessie sat Tom down and started to find out the damage. She wanted to know everything, no more lies, no more deceit. They called in the accountants to sort out the books and the Brewery's auditors to assess the stock. More importantly Tom agreed to go on a course run by the Sallies dealing with alcoholics and problem gamblers. The jolt for him to stop pretending there was an issue was the hurt in Jessie's puffy eyes.

When the stocks were assessed, and the accounts completed the extent of Tom's losses were revealed. It made sense to sell their interest in the Black Swan. They didn't get the best price for it because of the uncertainties surrounding the books but it was sufficient to pay off their debts and leave a little left over for them, less than they'd started out with.

And so, Jessie and Tom have rented a house while Tom completes his course with the Sallies. Jessie meanwhile has gone back to working at a bank. She says Tom is making really good progress and they hope one day to look at maybe running a country pub but only if he's really conquered his addictions."

"Good luck to them," said Ducka, "I wish them all the best. And now my old friend it's time to wish you all the best." With the final mouthful of beer, Ducka looked at Sean, "'Til the next time."

Sean raised his almost empty glass, "'Til the next time."

Chapter Eleven

Stella

After the train crossed over the River Tees at Croft it began to slow down and Stella started to gather her bits and pieces together. She grabbed her suitcase and headed towards the door ready for getting off the train once it had stopped at Bank Top station, platform four. She wasn't sure how she felt. What was it about certain railway stations that seemed to create so many mixed emotions? She remembered the conflicting sense of sadness and exhilaration when, all those years ago, she had boarded a train on platform one to the rest of her life.

Returning to Darlington she had a sense of nostalgia and pilgrimage but blowing through the carriage door window was a feeling of unfinished business. This sent a shiver down her spine.

In the good old days, she would have caught another train to her destination, but, thanks to Dr Beeching, that line and many others had long since gone along with Darlo's railway workshops. So, she walked through the underpass to the road that led downhill to the bus station. The walk was too short for a taxi but long enough to be annoying.

As she waited for her bus, she wondered why Darlington had become Darlo, it sounded like one of those lazy Australian contractions. If it was meant to provoke familial affection it didn't seem to work. It gave her more of a feeling of a Castlemaine pub on a Sunday morning. Where was the wretched bus?

As she waited, her thoughts suddenly turned to Don whom she'd met when she was working in Munich, he was originally from Darlington. Isn't the mind weird she thought to herself, where did that thought suddenly come from? What was the nickname he told me that he once had? That was it Duck, Donald Duck. No, no, Ducka, that was it. Apparently from the hairstyle he used to have before I met him. Probably just as well he'd changed as greasy hair was not one of her turn-ons. He was a nice lad, but she'd left him in the lurch when she was asked to urgently fly out to the Athens office as they had got themselves into a pickle. She was in Munich one morning and in Athens that evening. She didn't get a chance to explain or say goodbye. She hoped he'd met a lovely girl, got married and left his demons behind him.

At last Stella was on the bus for the final leg of her journey.

The bus comfortably climbed the hill at Skeeby which was a far cry from the old United buses which, when full to the gunwale, would struggle up it at a walking pace, their huffed-up windows obscuring the countryside. This evening she could see the houses and the village pub. She could even see the stars. Before she'd left home to dine upon the wonders of this world Pete had told her that apart from the Milky Way there was one maybe two other galaxies in the universe. Now it was believed there were billions. It was the sort of figure that Stella could not comprehend no matter how much she tried. She sympathised with some of the aboriginal communities she'd come across where they counted up to ten, twenty or maybe thirty but anything after that was just lots. She'd read that maybe there were other universes, she just hoped they'd confine it to the odd two or three. If there were billions of them and billions of galaxies and trillions of stars, she just knew it would make her brain hurt at the mere thought.

The bus eased into its stop in Richmond marketplace. The casual observer would have seen a woman in her mid-fifties alight and stand there with her suitcase by her side. She stood there long enough for the bus to take off and continue its journey. She looked around at the Georgian buildings surrounding the marketplace; she looked at the church in the middle, she looked almost in expectancy at the obelisk where the market cross used to be. Stella recalled that that was where they used to meet, where all of us used to meet. For all its familiarity, for some reason, she felt lost. Her journey back had been a long one. She cast her eyes down.

"My God, what have I done?" she thought to herself, "Why have I come back here? I've spent my life not going back, not repeating things, always moving on. If something was so great, so wonderful, so gorgeous, why tempt fate? The next time around it might not be so good. It's like repetitive humour, the first time you hear a joke it can be funny, after that you laugh out of politeness. And if something was so abysmal, why would you want to go back? Life's too short. Move on.

What am I doing here? Why come back to where I was born? Is it to remember my lovely childhood? Pay tribute to my parents, long since gone? See friends who will have long forgotten me? Is it to remember Pete, dear wonderful Peter? Strange, I only ever called him Peter if I was mad at him, maybe I should have used his nickname, Petesake, but that seemed to be something more between the boys than between Pete and me. Why am I here? I really don't know; I can't explain it. A bit like some of Pete's thoughts really. Clear as a starlit sky to him, but at times, as clear as the Swale in flood to the rest of us, dear Pete."

A voice cut through her introspective reverie, "Hi up, Stel. Long-time no see. What are you doing here?" in full flow and without waiting for an answer, the woman who had addressed Stella called out across the Square, "Hey up, Norm. Come here. See what the dog's just dragged in. How lovely to see you Stel".

Stella had just managed a quick "Hello, Jude," when Norm came gushing in.

"Stella, how do you do? Oh dear, that sounds like one of those Johnny Cash lyrics. But on the other hand, no it doesn't. Thought of changing your name to Sue, it'd work then. Give us a hug!"

Whilst Jude's eyes rolled to the top of her head, Norm moved to give Stella a hug but halfway through the movement he broke off and waved across the Square.

"Brian, Brian, look who we've got here. It's our Stella. Come and say hello."

A man came panting up, "I'll be buggered. It is. You're bloomin' right. It's our Stella. How are you?"

A woman's voice could be heard coming from Finkle St, a

lane leading off the Marketplace, "Brian, Brian, where are you? You trying to hide again? Brian. Brian."

Brian called in the direction of the lane, to his wife, Gladys, "Hey up Glad, it's our Stella."

"Who?" queried the still out of sight but closer Gladys.

"Our Stella."

"Who?" said the voice which was getting closer.

"Yer know, Stella. Come and say Hello."

Gladys came into the marketplace and without looking around ambled up to Brian.

"Who'd you say?"

"Here - our Stella!"

Gladys looked slowly at Stella. She looked her up and down in the way she reserved for door to door salesmen. "Hi up" she said in a very detached way.

"You don't recognise her do you?" said Brian, "It's Stella, you remember from school?"

Gladys looked at Stella more closely.

"Nay, never. It's not. It can't be. Are you sure? Is that really you Stella?" Her dourness disappeared like a ray of light from the sun as it suddenly breaks through the clouds. She threw her arms around Stella and gave her a big hug.

"All we need now is Pixie and Dixie and it'll be like old times." said Brian.

"Someone mention our names? Stella, what are you doing here? Where've you been? What have you been up to?" asked the newcomer, who was obviously Dixie.

Pixie gushed in "Oh Stella we've missed you. I know it's many a year now, but we've missed you. Welcome home."

"What a coincidence! But there's one missing. Where's Roger?" asked Norman.

"You mean Roger Francis, or leastwise that's what his

mother always called him in full. He'll be up on his beloved
moors or still looking for his true love," said Gladys.

"Or painting one of his weird paintings," said Norman.
"Have you come back for good or are you staying awhile?"

"I'm not sure how long I've come for, but a little while
anyway."

"Where are you staying?" asked Norman.

"The Black Lion."

"Oh, lordy, lordy, aren't we living it up? Come and stay with
us if you want," said Norman as he looked in Jude's direction for
confirmation that she was alright with his generosity.

"Thanks Norm, that's kind of you but I've booked in for
a week, maybe if I'm around after that I'll take you up on your
offer, if that's ok?" responded Stella.

It was agreed that they'd all meet for dinner the following
evening. Norman said he'd try and get hold of Rog and see if
he'd join them all.

∞

It was a night of reminiscences. Stella started the tone of
the dinner by noting that only Dixie seemed to have kept his
nickname from their teen years. "Why was it," she asked, "that
the nicknames seemed to be a boy thing back then?"

Brian explained with plenty of supportive agreement by
the other males.

"Us lads had started to notice that girls were girls and had
certain attractions. But we were nervous about how you went
about approaching the opposite sex. How did you go about
getting your first kiss and what would it be like? The School
Dance was coming up and we didn't want to be wall flowers
and so to help our street cred. we'd thought we'd give ourselves
staunch names. I don't know where the staunchness went as the

names we gave each other became self-deprecating. Des became Dixie because he'd said he fancied Pixie, Norman became Abnorman because we thought he was,"

Norman gave a snort at this point.

Brian continued, "I became Brains, just an anagram of my name, Roger became the dodger and of course Pete became Petesake which came from the usual response to one of his latest theories."

"As part of the bravado, I think it was you Dixie, who put a condom into my top pocket, and Pete's as well."

"That's right," said Dixie, "I'd found some in my dad's dressing gown pocket which came as a bit of a shock at the time. I couldn't imagine my folks doing it."

"How do you think you got here?" interrupted Norman.

"I know, I know. Anyway, I nicked a couple and stuck them into a couple of top pockets. All part of the bravado I suppose."

"The dance moves were all part of it but the flamboyant moves we practised in private never made it on to the dance floor. We were more like totem poles swaying in the wind. We did so want to be cool."

"What did you girls do?" asked Roger, breaking his silence.

"Did you all come together and plan what you were going to do?"

"Firstly," started Jude, "we had to decide if we were going at all. We weren't sure what the talent was going to be like."

"The talent," broke in Brian, "are you referring to us men?"

"You forget what a lot of spotty Herberts you were in those days! Yes, you lot. You don't think for one moment that you had much say in the matter, do you? Haven't you learnt by now?"

"So, what did you think of us all?"

"Not a lot."

"Charming!"

"You asked. Dixie, we thought could do with some more hormones to make him grow a bit bigger, but Pixie thought he was alright as he was. As for you Norman, remember that pompadoured wig smothered in Brylcreem that you sported on the top of your head? Just as well that I could see the positive side of that. I reckoned I was going to save on hand cream."

"Oh, yuk!"

"I also thought he might be trainable." At which Norman did an impression of a begging dog to everyone's amusement.

"Pete" Jude continued, "was so full of his theories and books we thought he was like a walking encyclopaedia. Fine if you wanted a soporific. Although, I have to say we weren't all in agreement there. Both Stella and Glad leapt to his defence. Who have we left? Brian and Roger. Roger was quiet, a bit too quiet for us in those days and as for you Brian I don't think I need say."

"I know," said Brian, "the spots and the impetigo didn't help."

"But apart from that," said Jude, "you were fine."

Norman butted in, "Well I have to say your female charms hadn't totally been lost on us lads, Roger fancied Stella, Pete, I seem to recall was suffering from one of his headaches and viewed it all with distain saying it wasn't a meat market. But one of us pointed out that it was a M-E-E-T market, spelling it out. The rest I think we know."

"I didn't know you fancied me," said Stella looking at Roger, "how sweet."

"That's because you were too busy google-eyeing Pete," said Gladys with a hint of harshness in her voice.

"Didn't the dance get off to a slow start?" broke in Jude, "We eyed each other up from opposite walls and things only slowly got underway when some of us girls started dancing with each other. I think this would have gone on for the night if Dixie hadn't approached Pixie. After that you lads came over and we had great fun dancing with each other but by the end we had all paired off apart from you Roger, there were a couple of girls there who fancied you but you weren't for the tempting."

Roger silently acknowledged Jude.

"It's interesting," said Dixie, "that one night affected all our destinies."

"Too true," said Pixie, "and we all tried to put the world to rights that night. Can you recall we all walked along to Easby Abbey after the dance? Being a school dance, it ended early and none of us wanted to go home straight away."

"We all sat around sharing our dreams," chimed in Jude, "All but you Roger. I remember you saying, 'my dreams are my dreams.' And we sat around Pete talking about whether there was a creator. You on one side of him Stella and Glad, you were on the other."

"I started it," said Stella, "it was such a beautiful night. I lay back and looked up at that clear sky. There were hundreds of pinpricks of light. I said, 'all of this must have a meaning, there must be a creator. It can't have come from nothing.' I suppose I was being rhetorical and hadn't reckoned on Pete. I'd pressed a button.

I remember Pete saying 'Maybe it did. Maybe that's exactly what it did, it could have all came from nothing, a total intense, dense, nothing. If anything cared to exist at that point in time it would be overwhelmed by the all-consuming nothing. It is that wonderful contradiction − it is everything but nothing.'

You tried to interrupt him, Norman," continued Stella, "you said something like, 'Dense? Intense? You talking about yourself?' I told you to leave him alone and asked Pete to carry on. He did just that, he continued. 'Into this nothing there was some sort of intervention, maybe an act of God, maybe a bit of Brian's forbear's dandruff floated in space and time and was sucked towards the nothingness. It coughed, it spluttered, and said, 'I'm not having that' and with one almighty explosion the universe was born. Or maybe this bundle of nothing found things a bit boring and it couldn't stand doing nothing anymore. In a huge outpouring of frustration and energy it became everything again.'

I asked him if it was a sort of Yin and Yang," continued Stella. Pete said. 'Sort of.' I, then, asked him if that meant that everything would shrink into nothing again? Pete told us it was possible. He said on one hand it could be like a genie being let out of a bottle and it would be impossible to put it back in again or maybe after the explosion everything will start to shrink again. Slowly to start with, a little here and a little there, areas of nothing that will suck in its close neighbours, letting nothing escape. Bit by bit these areas of nothing will merge, one with another, growing all-encompassing but smaller and denser until once again there is a total dense nothing left. It will revert to norm. You may recall Norm you wanted to know what that had to do with you. And you Roger told him not to scratch his head in case you started an explosion."

"I poured a coke over Pete's head," said Norman, "I told him that the only explosion around there was going to be him as I thought his brain was overheating, Poor Pete wasn't amused and you Stella told me to leave off."

"Pete did try to persist against the odds," said Brian, "He picked up that stick and tried to explain that most of it was nothing, just millions of atoms with electrons buzzing around them, all little planetary systems, largely made up of space. He wasn't impressed when I whacked him over the head with it and asked him if that felt like nothing."

"It wasn't long after that when we wandered off in our pairs as I recall," said Pixie, "although there was a bit of competition between Stella and Glad for Pete before Brian tempted Glad away. And you Roger had wandered off a bit earlier by yourself."

"I remember Pete saying he thought I was beautiful," said Stella.

"I queried him, 'Am I beautiful?' He replied, 'I said I think you are beautiful, I hope so, I don't know, I haven't known you long enough.' I had a sense that here was someone who was looking at me as a whole person, not just my boobs or bottom or legs. I think it was then I started to fall for him."

"You all quickly settled into your relationships and kindly let me play gooseberry when you went out walking or to the cinema. It's amazing how well matched you all were from the start," said Roger.

"That's as it may have appeared, but there were bumps in the road," said Jude. "Once, you can't have been there Roger, we were all going to the flicks. We agreed to meet in the marketplace. It must have been something in the wind, but we all seemed a bit fractious that day. It started with Pixie and Dixie. I think Dixie had objected to being called Dixie. Then Glad you got in on the act by making a reference to a condom in Pete's jacket pocket. That upset Stella. This was quickly followed by Brian being annoyed at you for trying to split Pete and Stella up. He was talking about dumping you, Glad. The only sane pair were Norman and me. We just looked at each other and wondered what we'd walked into. We were able to calm people down, but it was a very frosty visit to the cinema."

"I was sure mad with Pete and not feeling too loving towards him," said Stella, "but later he explained and any further discussion was forgotten as he came down with one of those dreadful migraines he used to suffer from, poor Pete."

"If we'd known better at the time I wonder if the outcome would have been different," mused Norman, "that last day of school is one we will always remember but more so for you Stella."

"Yes," said Stella, "school was finally over and behind us. Pete and I were all set to go to London, him to study physics and me, law. The world lay in front of us. We walked down to the waterfall and sat on the rocks and dreamt of our life beyond that. I don't think there was one part of the world that we didn't travel to in our imaginations. He had such an enquiring mind and seemed to see so much; he saw beauty in everything, he was so inquisitive. Pete told me how much he loved me and kept talking about all the things we were going to do. We lay back on the rocks letting the sun kiss us in our ecstasy. We were just so happy. Then, suddenly, he grabbed his head in pain and slumped back. Life became a blur for me."

"An aneurism, what a way to go," said Gladys sadly.

The dinner party came to a sober end. As they said their goodbyes, Roger promised to take Stella for a walk on the moors.

Stella retreated to her room still with the thoughts of that fatal day. Even at the funeral she still couldn't comprehend that Pete was dead, it just didn't seem right. In the days that followed she decided to fulfil her and Pete's dreams, University could wait.

Her mother didn't want to say goodbye to her on the day she was to leave, so they'd said goodbye the night before. She'd got dressed early on that chilly morning and had quietly left the house with her rucksack on her back. As she looked back towards the house, she saw her mother's bedroom curtain twitch.

Stella smiled as she remembered asking the bus driver for a single to the rest of the world. He'd replied that if Darlington was the rest of the world, then Lord help us love, but that was as far as he was going.

∞

The following day Roger took a day off work and picked up Stella from the hotel. He drove them up the dale and headed through Reeth and towards Tan Hill. He was very chirpy and as they went along, he told her about his love of the moors, his paintings, and that he worked for Mike Sheehan at Altberg, the best bootmakers in the world. He said he was really happy there. "And do you know Mike even runs chickens in the spare ground next to the factory and we all get our share of the eggs."

"How funny," said Stella, "I bought a pair of Altberg's boots in the Netherlands, they are great. I should have brought them on this trip. To think you might have helped make them for me."

As they tramped over the moors near Tan Hill, he reminded her not to wander too much from the path as there were old mine shafts littered about the place.

Stella was struck as to how infectious Roger's enthusiasm was as they looked at the vistas, listened to the curlews and heard the larks as they sang and soared to become pinpricks in the sky. Stella thought she knew the area pretty well from her youth but there were things about its geology that were new to her.

They had a wonderful day together punctuated by a meal at Reeth on the way back. Roger was working the next day, but Stella agreed to meet him in the evening and have a look at some of his paintings. She teased him about 'coming up to see his etchings' and smiled as he blushed. After a light kiss on the cheeks Stella returned to her room and slept the sleep of the just.

After a lazy start, the following morning Stella went for a wander around the shops and to pick up a couple of things she'd run out of. As she came out of the chemists she ran into Jude.

They gave each other a hug.

"How's it going then?" asked Jude in a conspiratorial way, "How did the walk with Roger go yesterday?"

"You nosey thing; but very well thank you," a somewhat amused Stella replied.

"You know, Stella, I've never seen Roger come so alive for such a long time. I'm sure he's been carrying a candle for you all these years. When you first went away you used to send postcards. Almost as regular as clockwork following their arrival he'd take off. It was if he'd been jolted with a cattle prod. He'd wander the world for a while and then return. One day he just stopped. He stayed. He became part of the hills and streams, part of the heather, as delicate as the nightingale, as camouflaged as the grouse. He became as much a part of the dale as the barns and stonewalls. If you asked him if he were going to travel again, all he would say was, 'When the postcards return' and shrug his shoulders."

"I don't know what to say," said Stella, "doesn't he have any girlfriends or anything?"

"He hasn't lived like a Trappist monk, he lives a contented life but there is a sense of something unfulfilled about him. It reminds me of something in you."

"Thanks for telling me Jude, I hadn't realised. I did enjoy yesterday with him but I'm not sure where it'll go."

"Good luck to the pair of you," said Jude, "by the way, why did you stop sending your postcards? Every now and then a piece of exotica came to Richmond, we enjoyed them."

"I thought that after I'd been away for a while people would have stopped bothering. Apart from which I became distracted by this chap I'd met and thought I liked. He was kind, considerate and a good cook to boot. But there came a point when I thought you could only have so many conversations about sandwiches."

"Sandwiches?" said Jude in amazement.

"Sandwiches!" emphasised Stella. "Anyway, I thought my postcards to you all was maybe a little like those sandwiches."

That evening Stella went to Roger's cottage to look at his paintings. They enjoyed a glass of wine with an antipasto that Roger had put together featuring some of the local cheeses that he knew Stella liked. She marvelled at Roger's composition and use of colours, they were so realistic, yet she could see why others may see them as abstracts. Time passed very quickly in each other's company. He walked her back to the hotel. They parted with a brief kiss on the lips.

Stella saw more of Roger over the next couple of days and thoroughly enjoyed being with him. She began to miss him when he wasn't there. The kiss on the lips had become more lingering. She began to wonder if she was being unkind. It had been nice to come back and see all her old friends, but the winds of unrest were stirring within her. She knew the world she hadn't seen was calling. Maybe one day she would settle down, maybe even in Richmond, but not now. She needed to move on and as much as she had come to really like Roger it seemed cruel to be building up his hopes when she knew she wasn't capable of settling down.

After breakfast on the sixth day after arriving in Richmond Stella plucked up the courage to do what she really knew she'd come for. She knew she'd been hesitant, even nervous and wasn't quite sure why. Maybe it was guilt, the guilt of the living.

She walked up to Pete's grave in the cemetery, it was good to see that it was well cared for and not neglected like some round about. She was alone, it was quiet, and it didn't feel stupid to start talking to the headstone.

"Well, Pete," Stella began, "I've been to see the world and taste life as fully as I can, I've lived our dreams with no regrets. I've seen the Pyramids and Machu Picchu; I've had boy soldiers put a gun to my head and dined in some of the finest restaurants in the world. I've lived to see some of your thoughts and ideas emerge as theories about black holes and big bangs. I don't think I've seen your idea of the big reversion to nothing appear anywhere, but maybe I just haven't read widely enough. But there's time yet, I've still got books to read and parts of the world to see. It's strange, I look at your grave and know by now there won't be much of you left. You'll have been eaten by worms, maggots, microbes, and bacteria. You will be nothing but a pile of bones, yet you will remain so much to so many people, including me."

Stella hadn't observed Gladys approach the grave.

"Hi Stella, saying hello to Pete?"

"I guess both a hello and au revoir," Stella said.

"You leaving again, so soon? That's sad. I'll be sorry to see you go. I wished we could have had a bit more time together. We were such good friends."

"Yes, we were such good friends," Stella said with some hesitation in her voice, "and I hope we still are, but one thing I never understood, one thing that has puzzled me over the years. We were so close, we did so much together. But what I have never understood is why – why on earth did you try to break me and Pete up? What was it?"

Gladys looked at Stella with some surprise, "You don't know? You really don't know? Couldn't you see? Didn't you realise? I was in love with Pete as well!"

"I didn't realise, but you had Brian."

Gladys hesitated, "I wanted them both. Yes, Brian was tall, handsome, muscular. He had certainty. He was safe. He'd have a job, buy me a house, have a nice car. He'd look after me. Remember that guy who tried to grab me? One punch from Brian – that's all it took. Those muscles allowed him to practise his press-ups on me until I cried for mercy, if you know what I mean. I wanted and still want all of these things, things I didn't think Pete could ever have given me."

"I still don't understand why, Gladys?" persisted Stella.

"Because Pete gave me dreams. He took me to worlds where Brian was an alien, worlds that were unknown, uncertain, places I was too frightened to go to by myself. Without him, I'm more frightened than ever. I loved him and miss him so much. And for all that, much as I wanted to, I never slept with him. I hoped, I tried to encourage him but once he met you, he only had eyes for you. I sometimes wonder what he would have been like."

"I'm pleased that we did become lovers before he died."

"I thought that was so," said Gladys, "but you never let on."

"No, it was something special just between Pete and me. He was gentle, loving, and kind. His kisses were like brushes of magic gossamer from the stars. He had such magical fingers, stroking and finding spots of elixir I didn't know existed. Finding total moments of ecstasy, moments where nothing else lived or mattered, such divine pleasure, until exhausted we'd slip into a slumber embraced in each other's arms and perfume."

Glady's sighed, "It sounds like I'll have to get Brian some lessons!"

Brian's voice suddenly boomed out, "I don't need lessons, I just need the opportunity!"

"How long have you been there?" asked a flustered Gladys.

"Most of the time," said Brian, "I usually follow you when you come up to the graveyard. – just to make sure you are safe. Just before you come up here you go quiet. You say you are going for a walk. But I know where you are going. I just like to see you safely there and back – at a distance."

"So, you heard?" asked Gladys quietly.

"I didn't need to hear, I've known all these years," said Brian, "It makes no difference to how I feel about you. Anyway, I liked the old bugger too, he was my mate as well. Come let me take you home and we'll leave Stella with our Pete."

That evening Stella went for a walk with Roger by the River Swale.

As they walked along Roger said, "I went looking for you after you left Richmond, you know?"

"I didn't know until talking with Jude a couple of days ago," said Jude, "she seemed to think you followed my postcards."

"True, when your postcards arrived, I'd try and go as soon as I could. I knew it was like searching for a needle in a haystack, but I just had to try. I'd turn up in Segovia or wherever and just walk the highways and byways hoping to bump into you. I saw some lovely places which I enjoyed but there was always the hope that you'd be there. I came back here always wishing you would turn up one day. I just had a sense I wanted to be with you. I've more than enjoyed these last few days with you, it's given me a sense of happiness I haven't known before. Do you think we could try and make a life together?"

Stella paused before answering. "I have enjoyed seeing you and spending time with you, but I don't think it will work out. You are so at home here, your cottage, being at one with the moors, a job you really enjoy, your contacts for selling your wonderful paintings, everything. And sorry, I'm not ready to settle down, there are still places I want to see, things I want to experience."

They both paused for a while. Stella continued, "Roger, you have to understand I am not an easy person to live with. Over the years I have had lovers, but all have gone. Some because I threw them out because they tried to control me and others who were so laid back they were forever horizontal. Some were sensitive and thoughtful, but no one had the same thirst as I have for all the colours, perfumes, and senses that the world has to offer. That sounds a bit dreadful; there weren't as many as all that, but I can't get away from the fact I'm a junkie for world experiences. I can't live here yet, maybe one day but even then, I don't know. It's just too cruel to tear you away from here. Sorry I just don't want to hurt you."

With that Stella quickly turned and walked away before Roger could utter another word.

∞

Stella didn't sleep well that night. On one hand she had a lovely sense of peace and of having laid a ghost to rest. She was pleased she had returned. On the other hand, however, she knew she'd hurt Roger, she hadn't wanted to. She could have been selfish and just knew Roger would have been everything she would want as a companion, a friend, maybe even as a lover, as she explored the rest of the world. He was really lovely and because of that, her conscience just would not let her wrench him away from a place he so obviously loved and seemed such a part of.

She was packed good and early in the morning and waiting at the bus stop in good time. She'd say her farewells by phone or letter later. She took one last look at the obelisk and Holy Trinity Church before boarding the bus.

"A single to the rest of the world," she said to the driver. It seemed a sort of good luck talisman to always say something like that.

"You'll have to change at Darlington then love."

She put her case in the rack and sat down, she felt sad and was looking down. Just as the bus started it suddenly braked and jerked the passengers forward.

"You silly bugger, what do you think you are doing," yelled the driver.

"Sorry, I couldn't miss the bus."

"Where are you going?"

"To the rest of my life."

"Darlington it is then, must be something in the water around here."

Roger came and sat beside Stella.

"I told you I was only here waiting for you to come back. And you came."

Stella smiled and took his hand.

Chapter Twelve
Trying to Turn the Clock Back

If Albert hadn't said anything maybe Sean might not have been doing what he was doing, but the truth is he'd have found some other reason to justify his actions. He wouldn't admit it to himself, he was living a pretence. He told himself it was just an afternoon out in the car driving through an attractive part of the North Yorkshire moors which he was doing because it was pretty. Yes, he was doing it for the enjoyment. He dismissed the voice in his head which told him it wasn't the first time he'd done this.

He paused by the Beggars Bridge something he had done more than once in the last few days. Would the beggar's happy ending rub off on him? The suitor spurned by his intended bride's father had gone away, made a fortune, returned, and built a bridge over the river so he could woo his intended bride and win her father over. And they all lived happily ever after. He wondered if he could build his metaphorical bridge to happiness.

Sean knew he could easily find Pru by just using the phone book but for some incomprehensible reason he'd fixed in his mind's eye that they needed to meet accidentally for there to be any chance of success. A bit like when they had first met when their cars had collided. There needed to be a sense of fate about it. He couldn't rationalise his thoughts. He would love to hear Pru's voice once again, but, after all these years, not over the phone. A call out of the blue just wasn't right.

Which is why Sean had spent more than one day in the past week driving up and down Eskdale hoping. He was driving along Carr Lane in Glaisdale, but it didn't look like fate was ever going to play its hand. It wasn't to be. He'd covered, more than once, every highway and byway, not that there were many highways, between Sleights and Commondale. He concluded that it wasn't going to happen. Even though he'd seen building sites with Carr Construction Limited hoardings he wondered if Pru had sold the company and moved on after Ken's death.

Feeling empty, Sean parked his car near Danby School. He was wasting his time. He'd soon have to return to his job in Yeovil and have to get on with his life. He was distracted by the noise of the children as they broke up for the day. They seemed unduly rumbustious and he raised his head out of vague curiosity as to what was going on. His eyes were caught not so much by the activity but by a youngster with curly red hair who was in the middle of the merriment. He felt lightheaded, unreal, a sense of shock. It was a déjà vu moment. The youngster reminded him so much of himself when he was young, but with more verve. Surely it couldn't be, surely it wasn't. Was fate going to smile on him at last?

Sean went home that evening and he dug out photos of himself when he was growing up. The more he stared the surer he was that the child he had seen was a spitting image of himself when younger.

He felt excited. Fate obviously needed a helping hand. He resorted to the phone book. In no time at all he had the address. The following day a discrete enquiry at the local shop at Danby confirmed that Pru's son was ginger haired and he walked out with directions to her house. He didn't notice the funny looks that followed him.

He waited until early afternoon of the following day before knocking on Pru's door. She opened the door.

"Hello, Sean, I thought it might be you."

"Really?"

"Yes, it's a small village and we keep an eye out for each other. Libby at the shop rang me to warn me there was red haired chap asking about me. I guessed it was you."

"I wasn't trying to spy on you," apologised Sean, "I was just wanting to make sure it was you."

"And that Bob was my son?" asked Pru in a slightly challenging way.

The conversation was not going as Sean had envisaged it. In his mind the 'How lovely to see you' would have quickly moved into a hug. And the embrace would have captured all the magic that they'd once felt. And the years in between since they last met would roll away into irrelevance. They'd pick up where they had last left off.

As he looked at her, he thought she was just as entrancing as he had remembered.

Pru invited him in and led him down a passage past the open door to an office with plans laid out on a desk and into a farmhouse kitchen.

"Coffee?" enquired Pru.

"Tea please, but only if you are going to have one," replied Sean.

Sean sat at a large table as Pru busied herself putting the kettle on the stove and getting some mugs out of a cupboard.

"I was sorry to hear about Ken," said Sean a little uneasily.

Pru hesitated in her tea making tasks and bowed her head.

"It was devastating, Sean, devastating. And so unnecessary." Pru was obviously upset. Sean rose from his chair with the thought of putting a comforting arm around her. Pru quickly moved away and turned her back to Sean. He sat down again.

"What happened?" asked Sean.

"Ken was always careful, so careful. He believed that death and injury on any building site was totally avoidable. He drilled safe practices into all who worked for him. He said that he never wanted to be responsible for anyone's death on one of his sites. He didn't want his people to lose any time or work through avoidable injury. He said it was in his employee's best interests for them to be safe and he recognised that it was in his interest as well." Pru paused as she fussed with the teapot. She continued in a much quieter voice. "So, goodness alone knows how he was crushed between the side of a bulldozer and a wall. The operator didn't know Ken was on the site, he just didn't see him. He was badly cut up by the accident, he regarded Ken as more of a friend than a boss. The poor chap's still receiving counselling." Pru paused to pass a cup of black tea to Sean before continuing.

"As for me and Bob? I don't know if you can imagine the impact of saying goodbye to someone in the morning for them never to return. Sean, I wouldn't wish it on my worst enemy."

Sean could feel Pru's pain. "I'm so, so sorry Pru. If there is anything I can do to help you ease your pain, just ask and I'll readily do it. But I have a sense there's nothing that either me or anybody else can do."

"Milk and sugar?" Pru asked by way of changing the subject.

"Black's fine, thanks," said Sean and took a slow sip.

"What's happened to Ken's business?" he enquired, "I see the company still seems to be active with his name on it."

"It's going great guns and has been my saviour, it's kept me busy. When Ken died, we had several jobs underway. I felt a responsibility for our clients as well as for the people we employ. With the help of Slim, Ken's right-hand man, we've kept the company running. As Ken's company grew, I started to look after its books which gave me a good knowledge of what it was all about. So, between me and Slim we are doing nicely. Thankfully, it also doesn't allow me time to feel sorry for myself." Pru paused again for a slight reflection. "And then there's Bob. I need to look after Bob."

"Forgive me mentioning it," said Sean, "but Bob looks awfully like me at his age."

Pru's eyes flared. Her voice became slightly louder and more emphatic, "Ken was and is Bob's father. He was an incredibly good, devoted, and loving father. So, keep any other thoughts you might have to yourself. If you've finished your tea, I think it's time you were leaving."

Sean was taken aback. "I'm sorry Pru, I didn't mean anything. I fell in love with you all those years ago and I've never fallen out of love with you. Until the time when you didn't run away with me, I thought you loved me too."

"I did love you Sean, but I also loved Ken. That was my painful dilemma, and I made my choice."

"My feelings have never changed; can't I see you again? Can't we go for a walk in Auckland Park once more?" pleaded Sean.

"No," said Pru, "you earlier asked if you could do anything to relieve my pain. Well there is. Please go now before Bob comes home and never, ever come here or see me again. Do you think I'd want Bob to wonder if his life has been a lie and that maybe Ken wasn't his true father? Bob couldn't have had a better father which makes his loss all the more painful. Sean, the answer is 'no', please leave."

After the front door closed Pru walked back to her kitchen table. She sat down with her head in her hands.

Sean returned to his car. The feelings of loss he'd felt all those years ago when he had sat beside Darlo Town Hall, realising that Pru wasn't going to run away with him, were the same feelings he had at that moment. With the same sense of reluctance and hollowness inside him he started his car.

Pru emerged from the bathroom in time for Bob's return home from school. She had refreshed her face in the cold water that had flushed away her tears.